MURDER AT BAYFIELD BEACH

A ROSE BLAIR MURDER MYSTERY

JUDY KEIGHTLEY

COZY HOUSE PRESS

COZY HOUSE PRESS
MAKE A DATE WITH MURDER

An Imprint for GracePoint Publishing (www.GracePointPublishing.com)

GracePoint Matrix, LLC
624 S. Cascade Ave
Suite 201
Colorado Springs, CO 80903
www.GracePointMatrix.com
Email: Admin@GracePointMatrix.com
SAN # 991-6032

ISBN-13: (Paperback) –978-1-951694-46-3
eISBN: (eBook) - 978-1-951694-45-6

Books may be purchased for educational, business, or sales promotional use.
For bulk order requests and price schedule contact:
Orders@GracePointPublishing.com

MAKE A DATE WITH MURDER...

Find Cozy House Press online to read more great cozy mysteries!

www.cozyhousepress.com

COZY HOUSE PRESS
MAKE A DATE WITH MURDER

INTRODUCTION

The Great Storm of 1913 can be compared to our Hurricane Sandy in 2012, when three different weather fronts all converged together. One from the South, one from the north-west, and the other moving over from across the Atlantic.

This same deadly combination in 1913 converged over the Great Lakes basin and the worst storm in living memory pummeled the region for four days. Starting on Saturday, November 8th, the storm raged on until November 12th.

After it was over, 244 bodies were found washed up on the beaches and at least 19 vessels went to their watery graves.

Almost 100 bodies were found on the beaches between Goderich and Bayfield alone. Two of the missing ships have yet to be found. One cargo ship, the Wexford, was discovered south of Bayfield and north of Grand Bend in the year 2000. The other two missing vessels still remain buried in the deep waters of Lake Huron.

The cargo ship featured in this novel, the 'Hydrus', was actually owned by the Interlake Steamship Company from Cleveland, Ohio. It had a keel length of 416 feet, a beam of 50 feet, and a gross weight of 4713 tons. It was built in 1903 and was mainly used to transport iron, but also some other cargo.

Twenty-four lives were lost aboard the Hydrus during the Great Storm of 1913. The ship to this day is still believed to be one of the two yet to be found.

PROLOGUE

BAYFIELD BEACH

The grave had been hastily dug into the side of the bluff just off the path to the beach. At first glance, it looked as if some children had been digging in the sand. The air was still, broken only by the sound of waves lapping against the broad stretch of sand below. Light was just breaking. If you were to look closely, you would see the faint outline of a hand exposed by the endeavors of some nocturnal creature.

Life was stirring in the village of Bayfield...

ONE

"Grandma, Grandma, please, please, please can we go to the beach?"

Abby stood in the hallway, little hands on her hips, her chubby legs encased in pink shorts with a matching pink polka-dot t-shirt, little feet nestled in pink Crocs and a floppy, pink hat perched incongruously on her cork-screwy, bouncy, blonde hair. Pretty in pink always came to Rose's mind whenever she looked at her granddaughter, who had worn pink for the whole of her four years.

"As soon as Grandpa is ready, darling, we'll go. Now where is your sister?"

"Ella's with Ben in the garden playing ball."

Rose looked out of the kitchen window and sure enough, there Ella was with Ben jumping in the air, tail wagging, big tongue hanging out, black coat glistening while Ella threw the ball in the air saying, "Fetch, Ben, fetch." What a contrast the two little girls made, total opposites, one blonde, fair and pink, the other raven haired, tanned brown as a berry, lean and pixie-like. At two, Ella was the picture of health and a tomboy at that.

When their mother had dropped them off to stay for the weekend, she had insisted that the girls get to bed by six and it was already four. Rose called out to the garage.

"Tom, are you ready? Abby is champing at the bit to go to the beach. Could you round up Ben and his leash while I get the girls ready?"

"I am ready, Grandma," Abby plaintively wailed. "I want to go to the beach."

Finally, all five were set. With Ben taking the lead, they walked along Bayfield Terrace to Pioneer Park.

"Oh, Grandma, look, I can see Grandpa's boat, there, in the water."

Abby pointed her chubby fingers out to the lake. The water sparkled as the sun's rays danced upon the surface. Two sailing boats lazily moved across, a gentle breeze just puffing the sails out like downy feathers.

"Silly Abby, that's not Grandpa's boat. His boat is in the Nina."

"You mean marina, darling, but you're quite right. Grandpa's boat is moored up. Maybe we might take you girls for a sail tomorrow. What do you say, Grandpa?"

Tom looked out at the lake, one large hand wrapped around Ella's little fingers and his other hand holding Ben's leash. At 58, he still had the ability to make Rose catch her breath and fall head over heels in love with her man. His eyes still twinkled, and his lips still held that sensuous promise, even though his hair had completely turned to grey and his face was lined and rugged. Tom and Rose had been childhood sweethearts. They had grown up and grown old together and now they were sharing the best time together since they had both retired and were grandparents.

"If there is enough wind, we'll take the boat out for a sail, but right now I'm going to race you two girls down to the beach."

With that, Tom let Ben off the leash whilst Ella and Abby scrambled to get ahead, the three of them tearing down the wooden steps to the sandy beach below. Rose watched as her family ran ahead. *How incredibly blessed I am*, she thought for the hundredth time, blessed to have so much. She set off down the steps to follow her family, knowing full well that they would be anxious to go into the lake.

"Grandma, Grandma, can we go in the water?" Abby shrieked and before Rose had time to answer she had pulled off her shorts and t-shirt, revealing a little pink bathing suit. Ella proceeded to do the same.

"Tom, where did Ben go?"

"Don't worry, darling, he likes to explore the beach. He'll be back when he's sniffed out all the smells."

"Yes, well, the last time we brought him here, he rolled in a dead fish and I had to shampoo him. Are you going into the water with the girls?"

Tom had rolled up his trousers and was knee deep in the water, with Abby and Ella splashing all around him. They were like fish and absolutely adored the lake.

Rose looked at her watch. They couldn't stay out too long if she was to keep the girls on their routine of a six o'clock bedtime. She had already prepared their dinner, Grandma's spaghetti pie, followed by chocolate cake and ice cream. Where was Ben? Rose scanned the beach, but the dog was nowhere in sight.

"Girls, you have just ten minutes before we have to go back

to the house. Tom, I'll watch the girls if you could go and find that naughty dog. You better take his leash. Here it is. You might have to drag him away from some smelly fish."

Tom rolled down his trousers and put on his sandals. Picking up the leash, he started off down the beach. Rose watched as he reached the first groin opposite the old shipwreck and she thought of all the tall tales she had told the girls about pirates and hidden treasure.

Abby broke her reverie with her plaintive little voice. "Grandma, can we please stay longer, please?"

"No, we have to get back. Now, let's dry off and sit here while we wait for Grandpa and Ben to return."

Rose patted the sand next to her, where she had placed a towel. Ella obligingly came to sit down, but Abby remained stubbornly knee deep in the water.

"Come on, Abby. Don't you want any of Grandma's spaghetti pie?"

Abby relented, and splashing the water with her feet, she trudged over to Rose and Ella.

"Where's Grandpa?"

"He went to fetch Ben. Look, I see him over there, and it looks like Ben's been digging."

Rose watched as Tom clipped the leash on Ben and attempted to drag the reluctant dog away. Suddenly Tom straightened his back and then stepped forward whilst peering intently at something. He then came running back, Ben in tow, calling out to Rose.

"Get my cell phone out of the bag and call the police."

Rose looked at her husband and saw that he was shocked, pale, and very frightened. She didn't want to alarm the girls. Calmly, she asked Tom if there was a problem. Maybe he might like to take the phone and make the call himself, preferably away from the children? She said that while pointedly looking at the girls.

"Oh, yes, darling, good idea. I'll just make my call. You had better stay here."

Tom walked a few yards away, and Rose strained her ears to hear what he was saying. She couldn't hear much as Abby and Ella started scrapping over who would carry the beach bag. Ella was determined to get her way as Abby had carried the bag down to the beach, so it was her turn now. Rose, as always, hit upon a compromise. "Abby can take Ben's leash and Ella can carry the bag. Now is everybody happy?"

Tom returned and whispered in Rose's ear, "The police are on their way. Ben uncovered a body on the beach. Don't say anything to the girls. Look, I'll stay here and you can take them back to the house."

"Oh, my gosh! A body!"

"Shhh. The girls will hear you. We'll talk when I get back."

Rose took Ella and Abby's hands and, as usual, Ben tugged at his leash, pulling Abby along. *A body on the beach*, Rose thought. *I didn't even ask Tom whether it was a man or a woman?*

A black car pulled into the car park and a tall, attractive woman got out. She was wearing casual jeans and a yellow t-shirt and had flip-flops on her tanned feet. She reached into the back seat of the car, pulled out a black leather bag, and stood looking out to the lake, scanning the horizon as if looking for a boat. Tom saw her from a distance.

He wasn't expecting anyone to arrive so quickly and if it hadn't been for the black, unmarked police car, he would never have guessed that the long legged beauty was, in fact, a police officer. She seemed to snap out of her reverie and walked over to Tom, extending her hand as she reached him.

"I'm Inspector Parker. Are you Tom? You're probably wondering how I got here so quickly. I'm technically on holiday. I work for the Serious Crimes Unit in London. When they got the call that a body had been found, I was contacted and here I am. Could you show me where you found the body?"

Tom led her pass where Rose and the children had been playing, over the groin, opposite the wreck and there, partially hidden in some undergrowth, a mound of what from a distance looked like a pile of clothes but on closer inspection proved to be the body of a man.

"Your dog found the body?" Inspector Parker asked, while opening her bag and pulling out some latex gloves, yellow tape, and some wooden pegs.

"It looks like your dog dug up the earth around the body. What sort of dog do you own?"

Tom answered as he watched her deftly put the pegs and tape all around the site where the body lay inert in the sand. She finished what she was doing and looked at her watch.

"You know something, let's sit down and have a chat. Nobody will be here for at least 30 minutes as they will be sending in a team from Exeter. Now, can you tell me your full name?"

Tom told her all that he could, which wasn't much, but he found her easy to talk to and a good listener. She wrote everything down in her notebook and concluded by saying, "You say that your wife's name is Rose? She wouldn't by any chance be Rose Tredle? I knew a Rose Tredle when I was at university and she used to speak about Bayfield way back then."

"Why yes, she married me and now is Rose Blair. So, you were good friends?"

"Yes, for four years we did everything together, and then we graduated and lost touch. I'd love to see Rose again. Could I come around after we've finished here?"

"Certainly, you've got our address in my statement. Hopefully our grandchildren will be in bed by then; I know that Rose will be thrilled to see an old friend from university days."

"Right, well, I'd better go and look at the body. You may go now. I have your address. I'll see you later."

Tom watched Inspector Parker for a moment while she stepped over the yellow tape, put on her latex gloves, and knelt down next to the body. From the little that he had observed, there appeared few signs of anything other than a natural death. If the body had not been half buried in the sand, then one could easily have thought that maybe the man had a heart attack and died on the beach.

The shallow grave, however, spoke of harsher things; Tom couldn't help but think that they were looking at murder.

It was actually two days before Inspector Parker got in touch with Rose.

TWO

"Rose, this is Susan Parker. Do you remember me?"

"Of course, I do. Tom told me that he had met you. How very exciting. I'm dying to catch up. What are you doing right now?"

"Well, that's what I'm phoning about; could we get together at The Black Dog, say in 20 minutes? I've got about one hour to spare before the next meeting. We've taken over the Lion's Hall for the investigation."

"Oh, yes, we heard on the news that it was definitely a case of murder, but the Lion's Hall? I can hardly imagine a murder investigation here in Bayfield and in the Lion's Hall, of all places. We meet there for our Historical Society meetings! Anyway, I cannot wait to hear all about the case and I'm free as our grandchildren have gone home. I'll see you soon."

With that, Rose put the phone down and immediately called Tom.

"Tom, was Susan really attractive? Has she aged well?" Rose had suddenly felt rather insecure about her looks. It had been over thirty years since she had last seen her friend and she herself had aged, filled out, gained quite a few grey hairs, not to mention wrinkles, which she preferred to call character lines. Tom looked at her and gave her a kiss.

"Don't worry, love, you run rings around her!"

The Black Dog was buzzing with people, both inside and outside. *What a wonderful pub,* Rose thought as she cycled up to the wrought-iron fence which fronted the patio and leant her bicycle against the railings. She scanned the outside tables and couldn't see anyone resembling Susan. Walking inside the pub, she had to adjust her eyes to the dark. The sun had been high over Main Street, but inside was cool and the light muted.

Sitting on a bar stool was a single woman with her back to the door. She was engaged in a conversation with the barman, but Rose knew immediately that it was Susan by the way she was gesticulating with her hands. They used to laugh at her dramatic way of talking with her hands flapping away this way and that.

Rose observed her friend from the door. She had short brown, impeccably cut hair, slightly wavy, layered and tapered in at the neck. She was wearing a light beige silk blouse with rust covered pants which covered her slim, long legs down to her elegant cream leather pumps.

Rose immediately felt underdressed in her green T-shirt and blue Capris with yellow canvas beach shoes. Even Rose's hair felt messy and unkempt compared to Susan's coiffured style. Rose walked up to Susan and tapped her lightly on her shoulder.

"Hi, Susan. I would have recognized you anywhere!"

"Rose, Rosemary Tredle, just look at you! You haven't

changed a bit. Come, give me a hug. This is so great meeting up with you after all these years."

Rose pulled up a bar stool and soon the years melted away, and it felt just like the old days, sitting in one of the many bars in Kingston, drinking with her old friend.

"So, are you married? Do you have children?" Rose peered at Susan's wedding finger where there was no sign of any ring.

"Well, I was married shortly after we graduated. I married Greg, a huge mistake. He was all wine and roses before our wedding and then afterwards it was as if I did not exist. Fortunately, we did not have any children. You know that I worked at Whitby High for six years, but after our divorce I wanted a change, a real change, so I left teaching and enrolled in the police academy."

Susan paused and took in a deep breath before continuing.

"Boy, the training was tough, and I had to put up with such chauvinistic behaviour from the rest of the faculty. There were only three women enrolled with me. All that male testosterone, but I qualified top of the class, which I'm very proud to say. It's been hard working in a predominantly male workplace, but I've loved my work. I retire next year, though. Quite frankly, that scares me but enough about me. What have you been doing with your life? I know that you've married Tom who, by the way, I think is lovely. What about your career?"

"Not nearly as exciting as yours, I'm afraid. I taught for thirty-two years, mostly in Clinton. Although the first ten years, when we were living in Brampton, I taught at various schools in between having three children, Jessica, Anne, and Paul. Tom and I both retired three years ago, and we built our house in Bayfield. Where do you live?"

"I'm based in London with The Serious Crimes Squad,

and I have a condo in Byron. I was in Sarnia for ten years, then in Forest, and now I think I'll stay in London. Just my two cats and I!"

"We have one rather overweight black Labrador called Ben and a cat called Ethan. We used to have three cats but now just old Ethan is left."

"Well, Rose, this has been lovely catching up on old times, but work really does call. Look, here's my business card with my cell number. I'm going to be here in Bayfield for quite a while. Actually, I'm staying at The Cottage Colony and was here on holiday when I received the call about the body. Tom was probably amazed at how quickly the police arrived at the scene."

"I gather that the man was definitely murdered? Rumours are just flying around the village. It would be good to know the real story so that I could scotch all those rumours."

Susan looked thoughtful and began to get ready to leave.

"I shouldn't really be discussing the case with you, Rose, but I can say that we are investigating a murder. We haven't released the man's name yet, but I will tell you that he was not local. Right, I'm already ten minutes late for my meeting. We'll get together soon, I promise, but I must rush now."

Susan grabbed her purse, gave Rose a quick hug, and left The Black Dog quickly. Rose followed her shortly after gulping down her glass of wine and got on her bike. She proceeded to cycle down Main Street to the library. She was in the middle of doing research in the archives room, although her mind was definitely on other things. Susan had given her much to think about.

Rose was researching a document tracking the Great

Storm of 1913. The Historical Society was putting together a map, plotting where the ships had gone down in the lake from Kincardine down to Sarnia. Over 300 lives had been lost and millions of dollars of cargo. Some boats had never been found, others had not been salvaged but left to rot either scattered on the beaches or in the shallow waters of the coastline.

She'd been volunteering her time in the archives for two years and felt quite comfortable sitting at the large, oak table with her laptop opened, surrounded by books, filing cabinets and various artifacts displayed on shelves and cabinets all around the room.

"Penny for your thoughts," Angela said as she poked her head around the door. Angela was Bayfield's wonderful librarian, a woman who knew everyone and was a valuable source of information for any village history. Angela had been born in Bayfield and her parents were old villagers, too. "You look very preoccupied. Is everything ok?"

Rose smiled at Angela and shook her head.

"Everything's just fine. I'm just thinking about the dead man Tom, or should I say, Ben, found on the beach. He wasn't local and apparently he was murdered. That should scotch some of the rumours flying about him being drowned or having had a heart attack. Oh dear, really, those scenarios would have been much better than a murder. It's really quite unbelievable that a murder should take place in sleepy, old Bayfield."

"Well, it's not the first murder to have happened in the village. There have been at least three that I can recall. You know, of course, about the murder at the Albion, the Elliot brothers, Fred and Harvey, but did you know about the murder of Eleanor Burns, the wife of the General Store owner and former Bayfield Reeve, James Burns? In 1909, she was found lying dead in her bed, gagged with a stocking tied tightly around her neck and bruising on her forehead. At first the cause of death at the inquest was declared suicide and there was apparently such an uproar over this that a second inquest was held. Dr. Woods concurred that although the bruising could have been self-inflicted, the strangulation could not have been. A verdict of murder by persons unknown was recorded. Oh, and there was another murder in the village, and I can actually remember this one as it took place in 1952, but the murderer wasn't convicted until 1961. I remember the newspapers being full of it."

Susan paused and flicked back her hair before continuing. "There was also a woman, Helen Kendall. She was actually murdered when the family was living in Tobermory. She was killed and buried up there by her husband and her children were privy to the horrific secret for 9 years. After his wife's so-called disappearance, Arthur Kendal moved his three children and his girlfriend's six children to Mill Road, near the Bayfield water tower on County road 3. Eventually the children told their terrible story, and their father was arrested. You know something? Now I'm thinking, I think that there was another body found on the beach way back in 1939, a man called Rit McDool. His body was found almost in the same place that our mystery man was found. It was battered and severely bruised and he was missing a boot and his jacket, including $400 which he had been paid and had stashed away in his pocket. The coroner said that his death was an accident, but many people believed that foul play was at hand and that Rit had been murdered by a person or persons unknown. So, you see, there were four murders that I can think of which took place here in Bayfield. By the way, Rose, Brian said that you were talking to Inspector Parker in The Black Dog. Is that where you got your information?"

Wow, thought Rose, *I've just come from The Black Dog and already the village is gossiping.*

Brian was Angela's husband. Rose had seen him sipping a pint at the bar. *I'd hate to be having an affair,* thought Rose. *How would one ever keep it secret?*

"Actually, the Inspector has turned out to be none other than one of my best friends from university days. We were at Queens together. Her name is Susan, and she is lovely. I'm quite jealous. She's so glamorous and I feel so frumpy compared to her. We just spent a delicious hour catching up on our lives. That's why I'm so preoccupied. I'm just trying to process everything. It's not every day that you get a blast from the past!"

"Oh, before I forget, Keith left this note for you. He said that you'll know what it's about?"

"Thanks Ang, I'd better get cracking on this."

Angela returned to the library, and Rose opened the note from Keith. He was the archivist for the historical society and an extremely efficient and dedicated one at that. Keith had just returned from a conference in Oakville, which had been all about preserving the past, and was now even keener than ever before to get everything digitized and recorded on the computer for posterity.

The note from Keith reminded Rose that there was to be a lecture on *The Great Storm* at the Goderich library the next evening.

Rose already knew about the talk. In fact, she had seen the film about *The Great Storm* at the museum and was debating whether she really wanted to see it again. Most of the research on the shipwrecks from the storm had already been catalogued. Rose had Googled the Great Storm of 1913 on Lake Huron and had been able to download a map showing the approximate location of over 50 ships.

Over the past 100 years, much had been written about the freak storm. All she had to do was re-work the map of the shipwrecks and attempt to label the ships' names and locations.

Rose couldn't focus on her work, so she decided to call it a day and go home and make a nice cup of tea. Tom should be back from his game of golf and she wanted to sit down in the comfort of their sun lounge and feel the sense of security that she always got from her home and husband. The murder had rocked her equilibrium, shaken her in a strange way. Plus, seeing Susan again after all these years had made Rose feel curiously unsettled.

I need Tom, she thought as she cycled down the street, turned right at The Little Inn, on to Catherine Street, and then to Bayfield Terrace and her lovely home.

Tom's car was in the driveway. *Good*, thought Rose as she leant her bicycle up against the side of their front veranda and opened the front door.

"Tom, I'm home," Rose called as she walked through to the kitchen. They had designed their house to be open plan with the kitchen open onto the living room and a wraparound veranda encircling the three sides of the building. In the summer, Tom and Rose spent most of their time on the veranda. They had put comfortable cane furniture and outside rugs on the deck. Rose found Tom asleep on the sofa.

Leaving him to his slumbers, she retreated back to the kitchen and put the kettle on for tea. Carrying the tray outside, she poured the tea into two china cups and, just as she was placing the cup down on the side table next to Tom, he woke up, stretched, and smiled at Rose.

"Perfect timing, I was dreaming of a nice cup of tea."

"How did your game go?"

"Well, Doug beat the three of us. His handicap has really improved this year. We went for a couple of drinks afterwards at the club house before heading back home. Oh boy, it's fatal drinking midday, always makes me so sleepy. How was your meeting with the good Inspector?"

"Oh, it was great catching up with Susan. Tom, I feel as if my life has been so boring compared to hers. Do you know that she is actually in charge of the Serious Crimes Unit in London? She is so glamorous, makes me feel positively frumpy compared to her!"

"Well, did you learn anything more about the mysterious body on the beach because I've got one big scoop for you!"

"Susan confirmed that it definitely is a case of murder most foul, and the victim is from somewhere outside of Bayfield. That's all she could tell me. I got the feeling that's all they actually know themselves."

"Well, I can tell you the name of the murdered man himself and where he's from. Jeff heard he was a scuba diver from Tobermory, owned his own business, and had been to Bayfield several times with his partner since June. They both stayed at The Little Inn. His name is, or should I say was, Ian Richards. How is that for sleuthing?"

"Tom, how could Jeff know all of that when the police know nothing?"

"You know what the village is like. I'm sure that the police have been put in the picture by now. Apparently, one of the waitresses at The Little Inn noticed that the men had not come down for breakfast or dinner for two days. In fact, she thought that they had checked out and then the body was found and she put two and two together and told Jeff and he told us."

"I'm going to contact Susan just in case she hasn't been put in the picture, as you say. A scuba diver? I wonder why he was in Bayfield. I don't think that it's particularly great for diving around here. I'll go and make that phone call to Susan before I forget."

THREE

Susan rolled over and kissed Jim's neck while running her fingers down his bare back. She glanced at the bedside clock, 7.00 a.m.. It would soon be time to get up, shower, and start the working day. She looked around the little bedroom of the cabin.

Although tiny, it was so cozy. She loved the pine wood-paneled walls, the ceiling, and the blue and white quilted bedcover. In fact, she loved everything about the rustic cabins of The Cottage Colony, everything but the communal wash-rooms and shower stalls.

If the investigation continued too long, she would probably have to find something more practical, particularly when Jim went back to Wingham, back to his work and his wife and children.

Susan shivered whenever she thought of the affair she was having with a married man.

How and why did she ever get tangled up with Jim? Why could she not end it when every nerve in her body cried out to her that it was wrong and crazy to keep up a relationship which was doomed from the start?

But keep up, they had and had done so for the past year, stealing nights in motels or when Jim was supposedly on business in London. Steamy nights in her condo and now this - ten glorious stolen nights together in Bayfield where Jim kept his boat. His wife thought that he was sailing with friends up to Georgian Bay. She had taken their teenage children up to visit her parents in Quebec, leaving Jim and Susan free to sail and have amazing sex whenever they so desired. Well, until the dead body was found and it had changed everything.

"I'm off to work now, honey. I'll try to pop back at lunch, but don't wait around for me. We could have dinner at The Docks tonight if you like?"

Jim rolled over and grabbed Susan by her arm and pulled her close to him while smothering her with kisses.

"Come back to bed, Susie. We've got some unfinished business to attend to. Come on, work can wait."

"No, Jim, it can't. I've got a briefing at 8:00 and the Chief Superintendent is paying us a visit. I've got tons of work to do before he arrives. Bye now, love, see you later."

Susan hastily straightened out her jacket and pulled her pants back up. She was wearing what she referred to as her power-house clothes - a navy-blue pant suit, white silk blouse, and a red scarf tied around her neck. She closed the cottage door and walked over to where she had parked her car, a standard issue black Ventura. She would have loved to have gone back to bed and to have cuddled up to Jim, then make deep, passionate love. After all, what would it matter if she was a bit late for the briefing?

This damn work ethic of mine, Susan thought as she drove

past The Dock's and over the bridge, past the LCBO, and then turned right down Clan Gregor Square, past The Town Hall and then left to the Lion's Hall. There were at least ten cars parked outside.

Everyone's on time, she thought as she parked her car next to the Fire Hall and hopped out.

The smell of coffee greeted her as she walked into the room. Sergeant Flowers had already got the white board up and the projector screen down. All Susan had to do was set up her laptop and get the meeting started. She scanned the room quickly to see if the Chief Inspector had arrived, but there was no sign of him. He had told her not to wait, but to start the meeting without him. He would get there when he could. *Good*, Susan thought, *I can at least shake this sleepy lot up before he arrives.*

"Good morning everybody! Another day here in paradise! Now listen up...." Susan proceeded to tell them about the Chief's impending visit and how she wanted them all to look professional and, more importantly, to act that way.

"Right, Sergeant, let's get down to business. Here we have a photograph of the deceased whom we now have identified as Ian Richards from Tobermory. He was a scuba diving instructor with his own company called *Diva Diving School.* His business partner, one Sam Pierce, was also registered at The Little Inn and he is our first priority now. We need to find him and find him fast. Mr. Pierce will be able to answer many questions, particularly what they were actually doing here in Bayfield? Both men's families have been contacted. Mr. Pierce's girlfriend in Lion's Head hasn't heard from Sam for one week. She said that both men were sizing Bayfield up as a potential location for another diving school. The men met in

The British Virgin Islands ten years ago while scuba diving." Susan picked up her notebook and began to read what she had written to the team.

"Sam grew up in Wiarton and Ian in Lion's Head. Ian leaves a wife and two children. According to his grieving wife, everything was going well with his business. He had no financial worries, and she is perplexed why he would be even considering setting up another diving business in Bayfield."

She put her notebook down and looked at her team. "Sergeant Flowers and Constable Mathieson conducted a thorough search of the room that the men were staying in at the Little Inn. Sergeant, could you brief us with what you found?"

Sergeant Flowers looked like a schoolboy, although he had been policing for over ten years and was a married man with two children. His boyish looks masked a seriousness and dedication to his field. "Thorough" was his middle name. He had a soft voice but an easy to listen to way of talking.

"Constable Mathieson and I retrieved the keys to room number 8 at The Little Inn. Inside everything appeared ship shape until we realized that it was just a little too tidy for two men sharing a room. We found no computers, no briefcases, and no evidence at all that these men were here on business. We did find some scuba diving equipment, a double set. One other item of note was a booklet called *The Great Storm of 1913*, with a Goderich Museum stamp on the cover. A set of car keys was found on the dressing table and these we later found belonged to a silver BMW parked outside the Inn, registration number JMK 637."

"Thank you, Sergeant. Now that the coroner has sent us his preliminary report, it appears that death was due to strangulation." Susan clicked on her computer. "Strangulation and suffocation! Here and here show distinctive marks that look to be caused by a chain. Sergeant Flowers, come over and stand while I demonstrate how we think the death took place. Oh, can I use your belt?"

Susan took the belt and crept up behind the Sergeant while at the same time she withdrew a plastic shopping bag from her jacket pocket. Slipping the belt around the Sergeant's neck, she tugged hard and at the same time pulled the plastic bag over his head.

"There, now visualize a thin chain instead of the belt and imagine the strength of a man and then we have a possible case scenario." She removed the bag from his head and let him step away. "Sergeant, have you had the trunk of the BMW and the rest of the car searched for forensic evidence?"

"Yes, we've sent all that we found off to London but were told that we wouldn't get any results for another 4 or 5 days, though I can tell you that we found what looked distinctly like blood stains on the back seat of the car."

"Right, thank you. Now team, it's imperative that we find Sam Pierce as soon as possible. We have a recent photograph of the man supplied by his girlfriend. I've sent copies to all the surrounding counties, and as I speak, the OPP are out in the village showing pictures to everyone. We're trying to track his and Ian's movements since Tuesday evening when they were both last seen eating dinner at The Little Inn. The time of death of the deceased appears to be somewhere between 2:00 am and 4:00 am on Wednesday morning, a good seven hours after they had dinner in the restaurant. Where did both men go after the meal? Did they meet up with anyone? Good detective work is needed and thorough policing. Go to it everyone, leave no rock unturned, and report back here tomorrow morning at the same time."

Susan cleared her papers and closed her laptop. There was no sign of the Chief Superintendent, but that wasn't unusual, as more often than not, he got called away on business at the last minute. The team dispersed quietly, leaving Susan deep in thought.

Rose looked at her watch. 3:30 p.m. She had been absorbed in her research and hadn't realized the time. She always found so much to read when she was in the archives room, and today she had been totally focused on the Great Storm of 1913.

What a tragic tale of loss and what a freak storm it had been. Ten local families had been affected by the loss of lives. To lose the wage earner in those days before welfare and social benefits was nothing short of disastrous, particularly if the wage earner was the father of a young family.

How did they manage? Rose thought. The community would help out wherever possible, but it must have been incredibly difficult on everyone. Bayfield was, in those days, mostly just a fishing village. There were a few cottage industries but very little work for women folk.

The wives of the fishermen helped with cleaning and selling the fish, kept chickens, and scraped a living off the land with small holdings growing vegetables in the summer. Compared to present day, life in 1913 had to have been tough.

We don't know we're born, thought Rose as she packed up her laptop and prepared to leave the archives building to cycle home.

Rose wound her way down Main Street trying to avoid the shoppers crossing the road, mainly women out for the day who came to Bayfield to make the rounds of the fabulous dress stores and gift shops, not to mention the great restaurants. It was a beautiful August day. There was an absolutely clear, azure sky so, instead of turning right onto Catherine Street, Rose decided to cycle straight ahead to Pioneer Park, where she left her bike propped up against the fence and walked into the park. Going over to the wooden viewing platform, Rose stared out at the lake, which was as blue as the sky and as calm and smooth as a cotton sheet.

What a contrast it was to that fearful storm a hundred years ago when the lake had raged into a boiling cauldron of destructive water with waves over 30 feet high and water so icy that no man could have survived for long without perishing from hypothermia. Some ships had gone down not far from the shore and local people had rushed out to try to rescue them.

There were stories of extreme heroism where rescuers themselves had died trying to reach the sailors.

Rose had printed off an old map of the approximate location of the ships that had sunk in the storm. Holding it in her hands, she peered intently at the little circles and crosses that marked at interval spots in the lake between Kincardine and Port Franks. There were 3 crosses just south of Bayfield not far from the shore close to the end of Sugar Bush Road in what is known as Glitter Bay. Rose pulled out from her bag yet another sheet of printed paper giving a list of all the ships wrecked and what cargo they were carrying. There was the Argus: twenty-eight crew perished; James Carruthers, twenty-two perished; Hydrus: twenty-five perished; John McGear: twenty-eight perished. Then there was Charles Price where twenty-eight perished and the Regina where twenty perished. Isaac Scott was next with twenty-eight perished and the Wexford with twenty, perished. The Wexford was actually discovered in the year 2000, yet two of the ships lost had still not been found.

Historically, the storm had been called many names. It was referred to as The Big Blow, The Freshwater Fury, or The White Hurricane, being a blizzard with hurricane-force winds.

This occurred from November 7th through to November 10th, with the strongest winds on November 9th. In total, the storm killed over 250 people, destroyed 19 ships, and stranded 19 others. There was a financial loss of over $5 million, which by today's reckoning would be more like $100 million. The storm produced winds of over 90mph with waves over 30 feet high and white out snow squalls.

Rose shivered even though the August sun was still blisteringly hot with temperatures in the nineties, but the thought of the poor sailors freezing to death made Rose shudder. *Such an awful storm!*

"Right," she said out aloud. "No more maudlin thoughts. Time to go home to Tom," and with that, she retrieved her bicycle and continued on her journey down Bayfield Terrace to their home.

Rose always paused in front of their house and sighed. She adored her home with its rustic charm. Even though it was a new build, the decision to use old bricks and to have a cedar shake roof automatically rendered an established old-world charm to the building. Tom had built a white picket fence in the front and they had grown rambling roses, which were now in full flower and tumbled haphazardly all over the fence.

A fragrant honeysuckle vine grew over the front door and hummingbirds often buzzed by to suck the nectar from the golden trumpet flowers. Hostas acted as a border along the edge of the drive and red maples and hydrangeas framed the house like a picture set on an easel.

Home sweet home, Rose thought as she opened the front door.

Tom was busy in the kitchen feeding Ben, who sat patiently on the tiled floor watching him intently as he opened a can of dog food and spooned some over his kibbles.

"There you are Benny boy, now don't go and gulp it all down so fast!"

Ben had a voracious appetite. He'd once eaten a whole turkey one Thanksgiving when Rose had foolishly left it out on the countertop while they had all gone for a quick walk. On their return there was an empty platter, as clean as a whistle with absolutely no sign of the turkey ever having been there. That Thanksgiving the family ate all the trimmings, stuffing, potatoes, coleslaw, squash, and sweetcorn, but no meat, and the story of Ben's misadventure made up for it and had now been recorded in the way that all good family stories became legend; a folk tale, the day that Ben stole the turkey.

The fact that Ben had only been a puppy at the time had been forgotten, just as the fact that he had been as sick as a dog afterwards had been erased from everyone's memory.

Rose opened the fridge and wondered what she could cook for dinner that evening.

"Darling, do you fancy eating out tonight? I really don't feel like cooking."

"Yes, why not? Let's go to The Docks. We haven't been there for ages."

"Okay, well, that's settled. I'll phone and make a reservation."

Susan picked up her cell phone and called Jim. She was

running late, and it would make sense for Jim to meet her directly at The Dock's.

"Hi, Jim, look can I meet you down there? I'm running late and still have a few calls to make. Yes, 6:30, try to get a table outside, it's a lovely evening. See you soon."

She put her cell phone away and went back to the crime scene data plastered on the white board along with photographs of the dead man, Ian Richards. Blown up pictures of his neck showed bruising and little indentations marks made, Susan thought, by a thin chain one like a plug chain or a chain that held keys. They hadn't found any evidence other than inside the car where hair follicles, some skin scales, and traces of dried blood had been found. Fingerprints from both men had been detected inside and outside the car. Forensics had matched the fingerprints to both men, but the hair follicles and skin did not match the deceased.

The whereabouts and general movements of the men had finally been catalogued and pieced together like a jigsaw. From what people had reported, Ian Richards and his business partner, Sam Pierce, had checked into The Little Inn on Sunday evening at 6.15. According to his wife, Ian had picked up Sam and they had left Tobermory at 2:30pm which tied in with their 6:15pm arrival in Bayfield.

It appeared that both of the men had eaten dinner at The Little Inn and then left together at about 8:00 p.m.

Two men matching their description had been seen in Pioneer Park and one man matching Ian's description had been seen on the beach at around 9.00 p.m. He was spotted walking along the beach towards the old shipwreck, but no sign of Sam Pierce. He seemed to have disappeared into thin air.

Susan picked up the telephone log. Having received both

men's telephone numbers from their respective partners and even though neither cell phones had been found, they were able to trace all calls made to and from their cell phones. Interestingly, there were two phone calls to both men from the same unregistered cellphone. These calls were made the evening of the men's disappearance. None of this had made a dent in the police enquiries and already three days had passed since the body had been discovered on the beach. Why was Ian Richards murdered and who would have the motive and the opportunity to do this?

Leaving the Lion's Hall and incident room, Susan wearily got into her car and drove to The Docks. She was already 20 minutes late and Jim would be worried. Pulling into the car park Susan immediately noticed Rose's bicycle, and another bike propped up against the wall. She was always amazed to see how nobody padlocked their bicycles in Bayfield, whereas in London or Toronto, if your bicycle wasn't locked up, it would be stolen within minutes.

Entering The Docks, Susan scanned the restaurant for Jim. Not seeing him inside, she looked outside to the deck. Sure enough, sitting beneath an umbrella, beer in hand, sat Jim looking amazingly relaxed. Over in the far corner she could see Rose and Tom chatting away completely oblivious to their surroundings. She decided not to draw attention to herself and Jim; the fewer questions asked the better.

"Hi, darling." Jim got up and kissed Susan on her cheeks, "Did you have a good day?"

"Yes, well, not a lot of progress. It's really frustrating not knowing where Sam Pierce has gone. It's as if he's disappeared off the face of the earth."

"He could be anywhere by now, even across the border. Look, let's forget about work and enjoy the evening."

Susan smiled at Jim and grabbed the menu. She would try to forget about the case if only for one evening.

Rose and Tom enjoyed a good meal and were just getting up to leave when Rose saw Susan sitting with a man she did not recognize.

"Tom, look, there's Susan. Let's go and say hello."

They walked over to their table.

"Hi, Susan, you've met Tom before. We were just leaving but I'm glad that I saw you as I wanted to invite you around to dinner at our place. When would you like to come?"

"Oh, let me see, I've got a meeting in London tomorrow but what about on Thursday?"

"Sure, Thursday it is then, say, 6:30pm?"

At Susan's nod, Rose smiled. "Great! See you then."

Susan got out her Blackberry and proceeded to enter the time of the dinner. She looked up from her phone and realized that Rose and Tom were still standing there.

"Oh, excuse me; talk about rude, I never introduced you to my friend Jim. Jim, this is Rose, my old friend from university and her husband Tom. We've been reunited after 30 years."

Jim held out his hand to shake Rose's and Tom's. He smiled and shook their hands firmly.

"Any friends of Susan's are friends of mine. Pleased to meet you both."

Tom looked at his watch and then at Rose.

"Sorry everyone, football calls. We must go, it's the Toronto Argonauts against the Hamilton Cats. Can't miss the game. See you soon, Susan, Jim."

Rose waved as they left the restaurant. Cycling over the bridge and turning right onto Short Hill, Rose reflected on their brief conversation with Susan and her friend Jim. Susan had seemed a bit on edge and not nearly as warm as when they had been talking at The Black Dog. Who was her friend Jim? Was he her boyfriend, and if so maybe she should be inviting him to dinner with Susan on Thursday? She would phone her later and establish the specifics of her relationship to Jim.

They cycled into their driveway and put their bicycles into the garage.

"Tom, I'm going to take Ben for a walk while you watch your game."

"Okay darling. You know that fellow with Susan, he seems vaguely familiar. I'm sure that I've met him somewhere before."

"It will come to you, love. I also think that I've met him before but can't for the life of me remember where. Maybe he's got one of those memorable faces or perhaps he looks like someone we've seen on television? Oh well, I'll be back later. See you."

Rose called Ben and clipped his leash onto his collar. Tucking a plastic bag into her pocket, she set off at a firm pace with Ben as usual leading the way. They turned right down Mara Street and started to walk down the steep, shaded pathway that, incredibly, over one hundred years ago had housed a narrow-gauge railway which transported grain from the top of the bluff down to the port below.

Rose had been reading about the commercial enterprise spearheaded by James Gairdner and Tudor Marks way back in the 1850s. Apparently in 1856, over 100,000 bushels of wheat had been shipped from Bayfield, which was quite an amazing feat for a small village the size of Bayfield.

They emerged into the evening sun from the dark, leafy canopy of Mara Street and onto Long Hill and the marina. There were many large sailing boats interspersed with some very expensive yachts moored up at the marina. They walked down to the beach and as there were so few people about, Rose unleashed Ben and he went charging ahead and straight into the water. Rose rolled up her jeans and paddled in the lake whilst deep in thought.

Where had she seen Jim before?

FOUR

The task force was sitting around the board table in the conference room of the Lion's Hall. The forensics report had finally come in plus some further information regarding the sighting of the silver BMW registered to Ian Richards.

"Now everyone, listen up, this is where we are currently with our investigations. The post-mortem report has confirmed the time of death to be between 2:00 a.m. and 4:00 a.m., which ties in with the fact that the men ate dinner at The Little Inn that evening. They ate chicken, potatoes, broccoli, and carrots, remains of which were found in the digestive tract, and at least two units of alcohol were consumed."

Susan paused as she reached for a small packet placed on the table beside her. She removed a plug attached to a long chain. Dangling it from her fingers she proceeded to talk.

"A lightweight chain found in any hardware store, which one might use for a sink plug, like this one, was used to strangle the victim and, finally, suffocation took place, in all likelihood by a plastic bag being thrown over the victim's head. Neither the chain, nor the plastic bag, have been found. The blood stains, hair follicles, and skin flakes found in the BMW have been matched with DNA samples acquired from the home of Sam Pierce who, as we all know, is still missing. Both men received phone calls from an unregistered cell phone within an hour of each other. Unfortunately, it is almost impossible to trace the location of any unregistered phones, although we do know that the calls originated locally. Now, over to the silver BMW. Sergeant Flowers and Constable Mathieson extended their search and two people, one from Grand Bend and the other from Port Franks, say that they saw the vehicle in question and one man could even verify the license plate number. In Grand Bend, at around 10:00p.m., the car was seen parked on River Street, and in Port Franks it was seen at around midnight."

Susan walked over to the white board and proceeded to write down the license plate number and the time, 10:00 pm, Grand Bend. She turned to her team pointing with the marker pen and saying seriously,

"These times are significant, as up until now, Ian Richards was reported being seen walking along the beach in Bayfield at around 9:00 p.m. Presuming that the car was driven by its owner, then we now know that Ian Richards was still alive in Port Franks at midnight. Gentlemen, we need more information and we need it soon before this case runs cold on us. I am going live on television tomorrow asking the public if they have information about the two men and their car. Hopefully this will jog someone's memory. There have to be some more sightings of these men as they were out and about for over six hours. Now, Sam Pierce was our priority, and he still is, although with his DNA all over the back seat of the car, we cannot dismiss the possibility that he, too, might have been murdered.

If this is the case, gentlemen, we could be looking for a third person. The public is the key to breaking this case. Someone, somewhere, must have seen these two men, and it is our job to search out and find this information. We will meet again at the same time tomorrow."

Susan sat down and looked at her watch. She had to be in London at 2:00 p.m. for the television interview and it was already 11:30 a.m. *No time for lunch,* she thought as she packed away her laptop and filled her leather bag with papers and a report for the Chief Inspector. She would, in all likelihood, not be back to Bayfield before six or seven that evening. Jim had gone out sailing today so she would have to go back to the cottage and leave him a note. Susan was just about to get into her car when the phone rang.

"Inspector Parker here, how can I help you?"

"Oh, Susan, you sound so very official. Look, it's just me, Rose, I wanted to ask you if your friend Jim might like to join us for dinner tomorrow night?"

Susan thought quickly. She didn't really want Rose to know about her affair with Jim. They had been reasonably discreet about being seen together, and other than the odd meal out, they had tried to avoid public places. Wingham wasn't nearly far enough away and there could easily be someone in the village who knew Jim from Wingham.

She replied slowly to Rose. "It's awfully kind of you, but Jim is off sailing today and I don't know his plans for tomorrow evening, but thanks so much for asking. I'll be round at your place at six-thirty. See you then, must dash."

She ended the call and sighed deeply. If only Jim wasn't a married man, she would have loved to have brought him over to Tom and Rose's house.

Arriving at the Cottage Colony, Susan parked her car and quickly scanned the boats moored at the slips. Jim's boat was gone, and it was a perfect day for sailing. Susan let herself into the cottage and immediately noticed that Jim had not cleared away the breakfast things. In fact, he had left the coffee pot switched on which was a decidedly dangerous thing to do in a small cottage. Susan noticed the empty space where Jim normally kept his scuba diving gear by the side of the stove.

Funny, she thought, he didn't mention anything about diving today. In fact, she had laughed when he had unpacked his gear the previous weekend as Bayfield wasn't exactly Georgian Bay. It wasn't known for its scuba diving. This train of thought led Susan to another. Had anyone checked the records of who had attended Ian's and Sam's Diving School during the past summer months?

She fumbled in her bag and pulled out her cell phone. Punching in Sergeant Flowers' number, she waited patiently only to get his voice mail.

After leaving a message asking Flowers to forward the past years' worth of clients attending the diving school, she scribbled a quick note to Jim, closed the cottage door but not before turning off the coffee pot. She drove speedily to London for her television interview.

FIVE

Tom had cooked dinner. Well, he had barbequed some delicious smoked pork chops that he had bought from the Mennonite market just outside of the village. Rose put together a mustard sauce using Greek yoghurt and mustard powder. She also made a potato, apple, and celery salad and baked a fresh peach crisp for dessert. After dinner was over, they cleared away their dishes and sat in their cozy sitting room, snuggled up together pleasantly, full from their dinner with a bottle of wine open on the coffee table.

Rose put the television on so that they could watch the CTV news. A few minutes later Susan's plea to the public came on.

"The good Inspector comes over very professionally." Tom remarked as Rose watched her friend intently.

"Do I really look much older than her, Tom?"

"Of course you don't, you look years younger!"

"Oh, Tom, you're a darling but I really think that Susan looks much more glamorous and sophisticated than I've ever looked even before we had children. Oh well, looks aren't everything. I'm so happily married to you, and we do have three wonderful children. Susan doesn't even have a husband let alone children. Talking of which, what did you think of her friend Jim? I did invite him to dinner tomorrow but Susan declined and said he was on his boat. It's still bugging me as I'm sure that I've met him before."

On the television, photographs of both Ian Richards and Sam Pierce were being flashed across the screen along with pictures of the silver BMW.

"I hope that this helps the investigation. I sense that they are struggling to find any clues and it's already been four days since Ben discovered the body."

Rose shivered at the thought and flicked off the news.

"Shall we watch a movie, Tom? I need to have something to distract me from this horrid murder. What about a Hugh Grant movie - *Love Actually*, or *Four Weddings and a Funeral?*"

Rose loved Hugh Grant and didn't mind seeing the same film repeatedly.

"Oh, either will do. You choose. I'll probably fall asleep halfway through it anyway!"

"Well, it's *Love Actually*. Rose pressed *play*. Just as the movie was starting the telephone rang. Rose picked up the phone and looked at the display.

"Tom, can you press pause while I take this call? It's Jessica and I'll be awhile talking to her I'm sure."

Tom grabbed the remote as Rose picked up the call.

"Mom, I've just been watching the news. You never told us about the body found on the beach! It must have been while the girls were staying with you. I hope that they didn't see anything. It's just so awful! I can't believe that someone was actually murdered in Bayfield of all places!"

Jessica was always so dramatic, thought Rose as she attempted to placate and assure her that the children had not witnessed anything disturbing and that Tom and she had been discreet.

"Have you spoken to Anne or Paul recently?" Rose changed the subject quickly by asking about her other two children. She had become a deft hand at steering her drama queen of a daughter away from potentially explosive subjects. Sometimes it felt as if she was walking on eggshells with Jessica, whereas with Anne it was like pulling teeth. She rarely telephoned or got in touch. If it wasn't for Facebook or talking to Jessica, Rose and Tom would never know what Anne was up to.

"I saw Anne a few days ago. She's pretty stressed out. She and Seth had a big argument over the weekend, and they've split up again. Honestly Mom, I don't know why she keeps going back to him, he's such a jerk!"

It was a mystery to Tom and Rose why their lovely, intelligent daughter could be so blind when it came to relationships. She seemed to be attracted to the wrong type of man and had been ever since going off to university.

Anne had a series of stormy relationships and Tom and Rose wondered when she would meet the right person who might bring her some happiness.

Rose sighed, "Really all a parent ever wanted was to see their child happy." In contrast, Paul, their youngest, had taken himself off to Japan after graduating and was currently teaching English to businessmen at the Toyota headquarters in Kyoto. Paul had met the cutest Japanese girl called Atsuko, and they had recently moved in together. They sounded blissfully happy and Rose and Tom planned to visit them at the end of the year.

Rose ended her conversation with Jessica and snuggled back up to Tom. They continued to watch Love Actually, in mutual silence. The credits at the end were just rolling when Rose suddenly remembered where she had seen Jim before.

"Tom, I knew I had met Jim before."

"What, who...?" Tom said as he groggily rubbed his eyes. As usual he had slept through most of the movie.

"You know, Jim, Susan's friend, the guy we met at The Docks?"

"Oh, that Jim," Tom said looking decidedly uninterested.

"Yes, it's been niggling me but now I remember. He came into The archives about two months ago right at the beginning of the summer. He wanted to know all about the 1913 storm. I remember he bought a copy of the booklet, thanked me, and went on his way. So, now I can relax, I know where I met him. Didn't you say that he seemed familiar to you?"

"Yes, I'm almost certain that I met him in Wingham years ago. If it's the Jim I'm thinking of, he runs a printing firm and used to publish a business magazine once a month. Of course, it may not be the same Jim."

"Right, well it's time for bed, love. It's been a long day. Come on Ben, time to go outside."

Tom got up from the sofa and Ben, who had been sleeping curled up on the rug, stretched his legs, shook his big head, and followed Tom out of the sitting room towards the back door. Rose switched off the table lamps and prepared for bed.

Susan drove back to Bayfield from London feeling thoroughly exhausted. It had been a long day starting with the television interview and then a continual string of meetings one after the other. It was past ten by the time that she pulled into the parking lot beside the Cottage Colony. The light was on in the living room. Jim was deeply engrossed in plotting some charts, and he didn't even hear Susan enter.

"Hi, darling, did you have a good sail?"

Jim looked startled as he looked up from the charts.

"Yes, perfect sailing conditions with just the right breeze."

"What are you plotting?" Susan asked, as she peered over his shoulder at the charts.

"Well, I got this booklet from the Historical Society. It's all about The Great Storm of 1913. It's the centennial year, one hundred years since the devastating storm. There are all sorts of activities planned in remembrance of the storm and all the lives lost. I took the boat down the coast following the route that those unfortunate ships followed the day of the storm. I sailed as far as Port Franks. It took me over five hours and then I sailed back. A long day for me too!"

"Did you go diving? I noticed your gear was missing."

"Wow, it sounds as if I'm being interrogated. Actually, I thought that I might practice some diving, but I didn't have time. It just took too long to get to Port Franks, besides, the water is far too deep around there. I was just checking the lake depths on these charts when you came in."

Jim pointed to a roll of brown parchment paper sitting on the small kitchen table.

"That looks awfully old. Where did you get it from?"

"A guy out on the highway, the one with all those antiques, he had a stack of shipping charts dating back to the 1800s and he said that I could borrow this for a few days."

"Jim, you've been diving for quite a while now, haven't you? Have you ever met Ian Richards or Sam Pierce before? I should imagine you divers must come across each other now and then?"

"No, I've never met them in person but I do know of the school they own and operate in Tobermory. Janet, the kids, and I used to go up to Tobermory quite regularly. That's where I learnt to dive all around the Flowerpot Islands. It's really quite beautiful."

"What about in the Caribbean? Ian and Sam met in the B.V.I.'s. Have you dived there too?"

"No, but I once had a fantastic week in Belize. The coral there is some of the most spectacular in the world. I dived off Tobacco Cays, and the colours were like looking at Joseph's Technicolor Dreamcoat, just amazing! But I tell you who I did meet down there. Jeff Sinclair who lives here in Bayfield. He was on a scuba diving holiday with his wife, June. I met up with him the other day and we had a pint together in The Albion. I hadn't realized it, but he has a boat down here. It's moored close by on the South Shore Marina."

"Oh well, it's good that you've made a few friends here. What a shame that our time together has been cut short because of this enquiry. Don't you have to go back home on Saturday?"

Jim took Susan's hand and kissed it.

"My darling, if only I could stay longer, but Janet will be back on Saturday and she will be expecting me and then I do have work on Monday. Look, I'll try to get down for the long weekend. I'm arranging for my boat to be hoisted out then so I will need to be here. Could you book this cottage, or will you be staying on here after I've left?"

"Oh, Jim, I don't know. I might just check into The Bayfield Village Inn. I hope that this will all be tied up in a week or so or it might all be transferred to the London office.

We don't seem to be making much headway with our enquiries although maybe after today's news cast it might have jogged someone's memory. We have so little to go on!"

Susan sat down wearily and Jim rubbed her neck. It had been a long day for both of them and it was time to go to bed. An early night was required.

SIX

"Alright everyone! Let's run through what we've got! Sergeant Flowers, can you report on the phone calls you've received since the CTV news information release?"

Susan handed over the chair to her sergeant. She was feeling incredibly tired, hadn't slept well, and was feeling very depressed both with all aspects of her daily life and the case at hand.

Sergeant Flowers took the floor.

"Okay. Since last night we have received thirty different phone calls, ten of which appear genuine, and four of which we are really interested in. First, at 12:40 a.m., a Mr. Mike Kelly reported seeing three men standing by the side of a silver BMW which was parked by the beach in Port Franks. Mr. Kelly was out walking his dog when he passed the three men two of whom match the description of Ian and Sam. He says that the men were in a heated discussion, but he couldn't make out what they were talking about. Secondly, at 1:20 a.m. three men were seen in Grand Bend by a Mrs. Thomson who just happened to be nursing her baby. She says that she looked out of her front bedroom window and saw a silver BMW drive past. She didn't get the car's registration number, but she did see three men inside the car."

Sergeant Flowers opened his notebook and began to read from it. "The third sighting was from The Hessenland Inn, and it was at 1:35 a.m. The manager was just locking up, as there had been a wedding party that evening and it had gone on rather longer than expected. He says that a silver BMW drove past the hotel and seemed to slow down. He could clearly see three men in the car.

Now the fourth, and probably the most important piece of information received this morning, was from a woman staying in The Robson Suites here in Bayfield. She claims to have seen a silver BMW drive slowly up to The Little Inn coming from the direction of the lake and then she saw one man get out of the car. She couldn't see his face or where he went afterwards, but the time was 2:30 a.m."

Susan got up from her chair and thanked the Sergeant for his report. She began to pace the floor while she spoke.

"Now we have a timeline, locations, and destination, we also have a third person on the scene. Let's look at this in sequence. At 6:30 p.m. the two men are seen eating dinner at The Little Inn.

At 8:30 p.m., just Ian was seen on the beach. The next sighting we have of the BMW is on River Street in Grand Bend at around 10:00 pm and then another sighting of the car in Port Franks at midnight. At 12:40 a.m. we are told that three men were seen arguing next to a silver BMW. Then, at 1:20 a.m. three men are seen driving in the BMW and just 15 minutes later the BMW is seen driving past The Hessenland Inn. Finally, the last sighting of the BMW was in Bayfield at approximately 2:30 a.m. but only one man was seen walking away from the vehicle. Gentlemen, we are looking for a third man. Let us hope that we strike lucky again with the public when they show the interview again on today's CTV news. It will also be posted on Canadanews.com as well as all the social media we have available. Are there any questions?"

There was a general air of despondency hanging over the team. They had so little to work on and so far few breaks. Although the sightings of the car allowed them to piece together the whereabouts of the men, it did very little else. The third man now added another dimension to the plot, but they were still no closer to determining a motive for the murder or murders. Everyone left the Lion's building in a subdued mood. Susan wanted to drive to Grand Bend and Port Franks herself just to orientate the route taken by the men. Just what were they doing? Who were they meeting? Why was Ian murdered and where was Sam? Was he even still alive?

Rose had decided to go to her fitness class that morning as she hadn't been to a class for a few weeks, and she really needed to keep on top of her health. Since turning fifty, the pounds had just started to creep on particularly around her belly and hips. Many of her friends had hip and knee replacements performed in the past year and she certainly did not want to fall victim to any surgery.

Tom and she, on the whole, were pretty fit. They walked a lot and belonged to the local trail association. Tom played golf and Rose swam in the lake most days in the summer and, of course, she cycled everywhere. Their biggest vice was eating good food. Rose loved to cook, and they both liked to entertain but it was no fun entertaining if one was on a diet. The fitness class beckoned three mornings a week from 9 to 10, one hour of solid aerobics performed to great music. Rose loved every minute of it even though her coordination skills were not brilliant.

She also did some of her best thinking when at the fitness class. Whilst jumping up and down she planned her menu for that night's dinner. She had forgotten to ask Susan if there was anything that she couldn't eat. However, chicken was always a good choice if you didn't know someone's taste. Rose had a tasty tarragon and orange chicken recipe she could make and serve with roasted sweet potatoes and fresh green beans.

For dessert she would whip up a lemon mousse and maybe a Bakewell tart with cheese and biscuits and port to end the meal.

They had some coconut shrimp in the freezer that she would serve as an appetizer at the beginning of the meal.

Tom was off playing golf with Jeff, Doug, and Jerry although Jeff had to leave early so their game would be curtailed around 1:00 p.m. Rose planned to go shopping after the fitness class and then she would go home to cook up a storm for that night's dinner.

Cooking had always been like therapy for Rose. In her teaching days she would often come home after a long day of teaching, throw off her shoes, make a cup of tea, and then bake a cake. Somehow baking seemed to relax her and soothe her soul. Today was no exception. Having done her shopping Rose now started to zest the lemons for the mousse and then whip up the egg whites. The chicken gently simmered in a golden bath of tarragon, mushrooms, onions, and orange. The potatoes were peeled, pastry for the tart was made and chilling in the fridge. She was ahead of herself, time to have a well-earned cup of tea.

Rose took her tea out to the sun lounge. Ben followed her like a shadow, ambling his big body down by her feet. The booklet on the Great Storm of 1913 lay open on the coffee table. Rose picked it up and started to read again the names of the ships lost in the storm. There was The Argus, Caruthers, Hydrus, McGear, S. Price, Regalia, Scott, and The Wexford although The Wexford had been found 80 years later. Rose looked at the map that she had been highlighting and followed the passage that the lost ships would have taken.

Three of the seven ships lost went down in the lake closest to Port Franks. Attempts to salvage the boats had been made but to no avail, it was thought that they had gone down in one of the deepest parts of Lake Huron.

Thoughts of shipwrecks made Rose think of the dead man found on the beach not far from Bayfield's own shipwreck. However, this wasn't really a wreck from The Great Storm or for that matter from any storm but instead was an old boat intentionally sunk to try to prevent erosion on the beach to act as a sort of gabion.

The children had loved the wreck. Anne used to dive off the upended helm of the rusty ship until the lake levels dropped significantly. Now you could almost walk out to the wreck. In fact, in the three years since Rose and Tom had moved to Bayfield, the lake level had dropped at least 30 centimetres. Tom permanently complained about the slip where their boat was docked. The marina would have to do some serious dredging before the next boating season as already many boats keels were practically scraping the bottom. Rose sighed and went back into the kitchen, got out her beautiful Moroccan lace tablecloth, and began to set the table for

dinner. By the time Tom returned from his game of golf everything was ready for their dinner party.

Susan arrived exactly on time bearing two bottles of wine.
"I couldn't decide whether to bring the Italian Chianti or the
Pelee Island Chardonnay, so I brought both. What a delight
your home is! It's adorable from the outside."

"Well, if you want to have a quick look around, I'll be more
than happy to show you. I'm not a house-proud person so you
have to take us as you find us!"

Rose took Susan through the house pointing out some
features, particularly the stained-glass window set into the top
half of their master bedroom window. Tom had found it at a
flea market just north of Goderich and it was truly spectacular.

They had also salvaged old wooden doors from a couple of
turn of the century houses that had been demolished in Exeter.
Combining the old with the new, the house still felt contempo-
rary but had the warmth and character normally associated
with an old cottage.

With the tour finished, they sat in the sun lounge while
Tom fixed them all pre-dinner drinks.

Susan and Rose chatted away like old friends. It felt as if
the years had melted away and they were once more back at
university and still young things in their twenties. Tom joined
them and they continued their easy going talk right through
dinner. It was while they were sipping their coffee that Rose
started to enquire about the case.

"We saw you on the television last night. Did you get
much response?"

Susan looked serious. "I really shouldn't be discussing the
case with anyone but honestly, we've had so little to go on it's
driving us all crazy!"

She leaned over and picked up *The Great Storm* booklet which had been sitting on the coffee table. "That's funny, I had completely forgotten about the copy of this booklet. The same one was found in the two men's bedroom at The Little Inn."

"Well, you know that this is the centennial of The Great Storm. This little booklet has been selling like hot cakes. We can't keep enough of them out on the shelves in The archives building."

"I wonder why two divers from Tobermory would be interested in The Great Storm of 1913?"

Tom looked up from his coffee saying, "It's pretty obvious to me; they would be interested in diving to find the shipwrecks. There were two ships completely lost, never found. If I was a diver, that's what I'd be looking for, the lost ships!"

Susan thought about it and then said, "That makes a lot of sense, Tom. You might very well be onto something there."

"Yes, well, I've been thinking about the case since watching you on television last night. You don't happen to have a photograph of the missing man, do you? There is something about him that's been niggling me. I'm sure that I've seen him somewhere before."

Susan opened her black leather bag and pulled out a folder. Extracting two photographs she put them both on the coffee table. Picking up one she handed it over to Tom.

"Here you are. Meet Sam Pierce."

Tom studied the photograph closely. "Yes, I'm sure it's the man I saw in The Albion drinking with my golfing partner, Jeff Sinclair."

"When was this, Tom?"

"Well, it must have been at least a couple of weeks ago, possibly the end of July. You could ask Jeff. In fact, I'll write down his number and you can get in touch with him yourself."

Rose studied both of the photographs carefully.

"Yes, I do remember this man. He came into the archives a couple of weeks ago. It was a Saturday, and he was most interested in The Great Storm booklet and the map I was working on. He bought a copy of the booklet and proceeded to chat away. So he is still missing?"

"Yes, and now it looks as if there is a third man in the picture, but thanks for the heads up on Sam. I'll most certainly follow up with Mr. Sinclair. It might be the big lead that we've been praying for. Thanks!"

Susan left shortly afterwards thanking Tom and Rose profusely for the lovely evening. She had a wistful look on her face as she departed saying, "You two are so lucky. I feel so jealous of everything that you both have. There you are so happily married living in this adorable house and what have I got? All I have to show for my 35 years is my career and half the time that sucks."

SEVEN

Susan walked into the Lion's Hall with a new sense of urgency. She felt it in her bones that the case had reached a turning point and she could hardly wait to get her team pumped up and ready to go.

"Good morning everyone. Now listen, we have some new information to help us with our line of enquiry. First, the booklet found in the men's bedroom at The Little Inn, can be traced back to when it was purchased from The Bayfield Archives the weekend of July 30th. A man matching Sam Pierce's photograph was seen buying the booklet. On the same day he was spotted having a pint of beer at The Albion with a local man, Jeff Sinclair, who lives on Victoria Street. I have contacted him but his wife says that he left early this morning for a sail. They own a boat and it's moored at the South Shore Marina. Sergeant Flowers, have you anything to report on the sightings of the BMW or any further information on the third man seen in the car?"

Sergeant Flowers stood up and took the floor. "Yes, ma'am. Yesterday we received another phone call reporting a sighting of the BMW this time with only one driver. At 2:20 a.m. a car was spotted in Jowett's Grove by a Mr. Dunn who had got up in the night to fetch a glass of water. He says that he was very surprised to see a car drive past his house at such a time. He says that there was just the one driver, but he couldn't get a good enough look at his face. He did, however, jot down the license plate number and that matches our BMW. We also received a list of all the clients of their diving school. Interestingly, Jeff Sinclair took scuba diving lessons back in June. Here is the complete list of clients. Lastly, we had a call from Sam Pierce's girlfriend in Lions Head. It appears she found a scrap of paper next to the telephone with a number written on it and circled in red. We have traced the number, and it belongs to none other than Jeff Sinclair. That concludes my report."

The Sergeant sat down and Susan stood up to speak.

"It is imperative that we interview Jeff Sinclair. I want one man stationed at the South Shore Marina and to wait for him to return from sailing. I will go around to his house and speak to his wife. The rest of you continue speaking to the public and keep showing them the photographs. Also, pop into The Albion and speak to the bar staff. It's amazing how much they can listen in to other people's conversations. It wouldn't hurt to do the same at The Black Dog too. So, get to it everyone. Today we will crack the case open. Well, at least we'll have a good try!"

The team dispersed and Susan put her laptop away and pulled out her cell phone. She was acutely aware that it would be her last night with Jim before he headed back to his family and his other life in Wingham. She punched in his cell number and waited for his reply. All she got was his voicemail.

"Hi, darling, let's have a quiet evening in tonight. I'll pick up some steaks and a salad and we can have a barbeque, or I'll cook them in the oven. Maybe we could go for an evening sail after we've eaten? See you about 6:00 p.m."

The thought of Jim leaving left her feeling so empty. She really should end the affair and move on. But to what? She had tried internet dating and that had been disastrous, even speed dating which had been hilarious, but she hadn't met a soul-mate yet. Most men felt threatened by her being a police-woman and when they found out that she was an Inspector a lot of her dates ran a mile. No, being single was lonely and Susan hated it.

After leaving her message she got in her car and drove the short distance it took to Victoria Street. She wanted to have a chat with Jeff Sinclair's wife, June. She knocked on the door and a pleasant looking woman probably in her late fifties with short grey hair and an endearing smile, opened the door.

"Hi, I'm Inspector Susan Parker with the Serious Crimes Unit in London. We're investigating the murder of Ian Richards. Could you spare a moment to have a chat with me?"

June looked a bit alarmed but beckoned Susan into her house saying, "I've just made a fresh pot of coffee, would you like to join me?"

She nodded and sat down in an immaculate living room. It looked like something out of House and Homes with all the colours coordinated, soft shades of peach mingled with sage green.

Very restful, Susan thought as she sipped her coffee.

"So, how can I help you, Inspector?"

"You can call me Susan to start with, but actually it was your husband I really wanted to talk to. Any idea when he will be back?"

"Well, he's gone sailing and could be out all day depending

on the wind. He most certainly will be back around dinner time. I'm sorry that I can't be more helpful."

"Did your husband take diving lessons with *Diva Diving School* in Tobermory?"

"Why yes, we all did but Jeff really fell for it, hook, line, and sinker, if you'll excuse the saying. We had gone to Belize the previous year and had our first taste of diving. The coral there is fantastic. Unfortunately, I accidentally touched some Lava Coral and got quite a severe burn on my hand. My diving days ended then."

"Mrs. Sinclair, do you know where your husband was last Saturday night?"

"Why yes, he was out with the lads drinking, I think at The Albion. I went to bed at around 10:00 p.m. and to be quite honest I'm not sure what time he got in."

"So, I believe that your husband knows a Mr. Sam Pierce? Can you recollect if he said anything about why the two men were down visiting Bayfield with their scuba equipment?"

"Well, yes, Jeff told me that they were here to look at some of the shipwrecks, you know the Great Storm of 1913. There were 5 ships lost in the lake, and I think that the men wanted to try to find them. Jeff was going to help them with the dives."

Susan looked at her watch and got up ready to leave.

"Thank you, Mrs. Sinclair, you've been most helpful. Hopefully your husband will be able to fill us in with some of the details, particularly the whereabouts of the shipwrecks. I'll leave you my card. Can you ask him to call me as soon as he gets back home?"

She went to the front door and once more scrutinized the interior. This would be the perfect living room for her if she ever bought a house.

Her condo in London was small and ergonomic but would never win any prizes on the interior design stakes.

One day, Susan thought, *I'll settle down in a quaint village like this and live happily ever after...*

In my dreams, she thought, *in my dreams.*

The weather was absolutely perfect for a sail. Rose and Tom had decided to pack a picnic lunch and take their boat, *Tranquility*, out for the day. Rose wanted to track the shipping route used by the bigger ships at the time of The Great Storm. The map that she had re-worked was quite comprehensive, and it showed not only water depths but also possible positions for the sunken ships.

Ben just loved to go sailing with them. He was a true sea-dog. Right from the minute that he jumped down from the jetty onto *Tranquility*, he would sit in the cockpit like a sentinel and would stay there for the duration of the sail. Even in rough water, Ben never left his post. He seemed content to sit and look out at the lake.

Steering the boat out of the mouth of the Bayfield River, past the pier, and into the majestic vista of Lake Huron, Rose always thought that it was like looking out at an ocean as you couldn't see the other side of the lake, the stretch of water being so vast. Sometimes you could see as far down the coast as Kettle Point where large boulders, 'kettles', dotted the point in shallow waters dangerous to any sailing vessels. Today the lake was calm, but already a northwesterly wind was blowing.

Tom headed out on a south westerly tack into the lake taking full advantage of the good northwesterly and doing a steady 5 knots. He had estimated it could take up to four hours to reach Port Franks providing that the wind held steady and didn't shift to a south westerly. They could always stop in at

Grand Bend for lunch, although Rose had packed sandwiches and a flask of coffee. It all depended on the winds.

The lake could be so fickle and change in a matter of minutes from being calm to rough. The power of nature could never be underestimated particularly when it came to sailing.

"Tom, my guess is that those men from *Diva Diving* came here to dive for those lost ships. It seems too much of a coincidence that they should be so interested in The Great Storm of 1913. I mean why else would anyone want to dive off the coastline of Lake Huron? What do you think?"

"Well, someone said that they were looking at Bayfield as a possible location to open up another *Diva Diving School*, although I would have thought that Grand Bend would be a better location. It gets a much younger tourist demographic. I can't see many people in Bayfield being interested in scuba diving, can you?"

"Oh, it takes all sorts, Tom, all sorts. You would be surprised at how many of our friends love scuba diving."

"It's not for me, love, not for me at all. I'd get claustrophobia from being under the water for too long. It scares me just thinking about it!"

Rose poured them both a cup of coffee from the flask and handed one to Tom. She opened up a Ziploc bag and pulled out a juicy bone for Ben. He never left his post but instead got down to a belly position and levered the bone carefully between his large paws, chewing it with great relish. Rose opened the pack of salmon sandwiches that she had made for their lunch.

"Here you are, skipper," she said, holding out a sandwich to Tom. "What a glorious day!"

The sun sparkled like a myriad of jewels over the turquoise blue water. Sometimes the lake looked positively picture-post-card perfect, yet there had been times when it had turned a scary dark grey, green, and even black all according to the weather changes. In the wintertime, the water froze around the coast. Icy waves made the beach look like something out of the arctic or like a moonscape. Winter was still at least three months away. Although there probably would only be about six week's worth of sailing left for the year, come October most of the boats had been hoisted out and put to bed for the winter. Tom had already booked for *Tranquillity* to be put away the week after Thanksgiving weekend.

Rose got out the map and traced her finger along the route the ships had taken one hundred years ago. The depth of the lake varied tremendously from around thirty feet to seven hundred feet and then there were treacherous sand bars dotted here and there in both shallow and deep water. None of the ships lost in 1913, over those three days of the storm, had gone to ground on a sandbar.

With waves of over thirty feet and winds of 90mph, not forgetting total white out conditions, the lost ships would probably have been overturned and battered by the hurricane-force winds. The loss of life and the cargo was unprecedented, and for weeks and months after the storm bodies and cargo had washed up on the shore all the way from Kincardine in the north, to Sarnia in the south.

Three hours into their sail the wind changed direction. Rose could see that Tom was struggling with the sails, his face was creased with concern. The lake had turned choppy and Rose feared for Ben still sitting at the helm, but the stubborn dog refused to move.

"Tom, I think that we should head for Grand Bend. We could be there in ten minutes if we turned the boat now."

"Yes, I'm going to change tack and turn the boat eastwards

towards the coast and Grand Bend. This southwesterly is getting stronger. We might be in for a rough ride. Hang onto Ben's collar. Here, I bought his leash with me. Clip this on and stay with him."

"I'll sit here and hold his leash. Gosh, but this weather has changed so quickly. Just look at those clouds. One hour ago I was looking up at a clear, blue sky and now horrid, grey, clouds have appeared."

They reached the Grand Bend docks on River Street and cruised into one of the visitor's slips.

Tom jumped off the boat and secured it by tying the rope to a post while Rose went off to find the harbour master to check in the boat. When she returned, Tom and Ben were sitting on a bench waiting for her.

"We might as well go and have a bite to eat and a drink. It will save you cooking tonight. Look, there's Purdy's Fish and chips or that lovely new restaurant. Let's see which one will take Ben as we can't leave him out here."

"We could shut him in the cabin," Rose said, looking a bit doubtful.

"Last time we did that we were told in no uncertain terms that he had barked incessantly. No, I'm sure one of those restaurants will be dog friendly."

As it turned out, Purdy's was fine about Ben and, as it hadn't started to rain, they were able to sit out on the patio overlooking the river and the boats. Ben sat under their table waiting for any 'bits' of fish to fall on the floor.

"I'm not very hungry, Tom. It's not that long since we ate our sandwiches. I'll just have a salad."

Tom ordered cod and chips for himself and a Caesar salad for Rose. They hadn't been there very long when they overheard a patron talking about a big explosion, and, as if on cue, a search and rescue helicopter appeared overhead. Rose called the waiter over and asked if he knew what was going on?

"Well, apparently a boat exploded off the shore just west of Port Franks. The search and rescue team from Trenton were called in to look for survivors. That's about all that I know right now."

"Oh, that's dreadful. I suppose nobody will know what caused the explosion? Has anyone any idea who was on the boat?"

"No, I'm sorry. We'll know soon enough though. Bad news always travels fast."

Tom and Rose finished eating their meal. Tom looked up the meteorological weather station on his iPad.

"The winds have settled down. I think we'll be able to make it back to Bayfield this time using the South Westerly to our advantage. With a bit of luck we should be back home in record time."

They managed to hit six knots on the return journey and, although the weather was still unpredictable, they reached Bayfield after only three hours. It was past six when they reached the cozy retreat of their living room. They were home barely ten minutes when the telephone began ringing. Tom answered it.

Rose was unpacking the picnic basket and had just fed Ben his dinner when Tom appeared looking quite shaken.

"Rose, I can hardly believe it. That was Doug on the phone. Jeff Sinclair was just blown up in his boat. That was the explosion we heard being talked about at the restaurant. I'm afraid that he is dead."

"Oh Tom, that's dreadful. Poor June. It's unbelievable and

to think that we almost witnessed the explosion. Oh, it's so awful."

"Well, we hardly witnessed the explosion. It had already happened by the time we got to the restaurant. It was the search and rescue helicopter that we saw."

"Poor, poor June," Rose said again. "I wonder if their children have been contacted. Don't they live in London?"

"Yes, both of their kids live in London. We should leave her to her grief tonight, but maybe you could make a casserole or something and we could take it round to her tomorrow. Doug said that June's neighbours are looking after her right now."

Both Rose and Tom quietly went about tidying up, both deep in thought. Although Rose didn't know Jeff well, she knew June through her Fitness class. She just couldn't stop thinking about the accident. Finally, they both sat down to watch television although only ten minutes later Rose got up and said that she couldn't concentrate on T.V. and that she would go to bed early.

Susan had received the call the previous evening at 5:20 p.m. The O.P.P. detachment in Grand Bend had been given notification that the owner of the boat that had exploded off the coast near Port Franks was a man from Bayfield called Jeff Sinclair. In her long career as a policewoman, breaking the dreadful news of the death of a loved one had never got easier. That evening was no exception.

Susan kept thinking back to earlier that day when she had sat in that bright sitting room chatting quite happily to June Sinclair, and now that poor woman's life had been irrevocably changed.

In her experience there was always the stunned silence after bad news had been spoken and then predictably a sense of disbelief, followed very rapidly by the stark realization and finality of death.

Some people took their grief quickly and stoically, whilst others wailed uncontrollably. Some even collapsed, but June Sinclair took the news of her husband's death with dignity.

She insisted that Susan stop and have a cup of coffee and while she had her back to her in the kitchen she asked in a small and shaking voice: "What happened? You say an explosion. Why would Jeff's boat explode? He's always been fastidious about anything mechanical. It doesn't make sense."

"We don't have any answers for you yet. Forensics and the pathology unit are looking into it. They are still trying to piece it all together."

The minute that the words were out of her mouth, Susan regretted it.

"Oh my gosh! Did they find Jeff in one piece? Oh, please say that he wasn't blown to pieces?"

Susan put her arms around the distraught woman. How could she tell her that his body parts had indeed been found, flung far and wide as a direct result of the explosion? Some things were best left unsaid.

After Susan had arranged for a neighbour to come and sit with June, she left and went home to Jim. When she opened the door to the cottage, she just crumpled into his arms, crying.

"Oh, Jim, I just had to break the news of her husband's death to such a nice lady, and I feel dreadful. You know this job just doesn't get any easier."

Jim held her tightly and finally they parted and Susan was able to see that Jim had set the little kitchen table with a nice cloth and a pretty vase of flowers sat in the centre. A delicious smell of garlic and onions greeted her and Susan looked over to the small cooker where she could see a beef stew bubbling away in a rich, aromatic sauce.

"Boeuf bourguignon, my darling. I know that it is our last night together, so I've cooked us a special meal. Now sit down while I pour us both a glass of your favourite wine, Chateau Neuf du Pap."

They had their dinner and then Jim suggested that they go for a sunset sail. The sky was just turning a deep purple and the setting sun appeared on the horizon in a flame of red and orange as Jim steered his boat down the river estuary and out into the open water of the lake. He killed the engine after they had left the pier, and then it was just peace and quiet other than the gentle lapping of water against the hull. They didn't go far, but it was enough to calm Susan's frazzled mind and relax her enough to appreciate the beauty of the shoreline.

Returning to the cottage an hour later, they both rushed inside. With the urgency and intensity of young lovers, they made deep and passionate love like there was no tomorrow. Susan clung to Jim and told him how much she loved him and Jim swore that he would try to find a way to make it work for them, but the minute that he uttered those words, Susan felt in her heart that it would not happen. He had never spoken of leaving his wife and somehow she knew that nothing would change.

The following morning, Jim hugged her as she left to go to the Lion's Hall. He seemed preoccupied, but promised to get in touch with her soon. She left with tears in her eyes. It truly sucked being the other woman.

EIGHT

Everyone was assembled at the Lion's Hall. Although it was a weekend, the team was still expected to work a case seven days a week until it was broken.

"Good morning everyone! We have had a preliminary report back from Port Franks regarding the explosion. Very little of the boat survived. They are still collecting pieces, but the severity of the explosion indicates something other than an accident or engine malfunction. We are regarding this as suspicious and possible sabotage. As to Jeff Sinclair, his body parts are still being washed up as we speak, a gruesome sight for anyone walking their dog, which was exactly what happened at 8:00 this morning when the torso was found on the beach at Port Franks. Pathology has this as well as other body parts and we will receive a detailed report from them in a few days."

Susan picked up the photograph of Jeff Sinclair and held it up for the team to see.

"Now, listen up, everyone. Jeff Sinclair was crucial to our enquiries. I feel that he could have answered many of our questions. What I want to know is, was he our third man or is there another person in the frame? We must show his photograph along with the two others of Ian and Sam to see if anyone can recognize the three of them together. The other issue that I wanted to discuss with you was the only connection that I can see between the three men other than diving, and that is the booklet on The Great Storm of 1913. It seems obvious to me that the two are connected. These men were looking to find something on one of the lost ships. I want us to connect the dots and find out what the motivations for their dives were and why one man, at least, was murdered and another blown up? Gentlemen, we have much work ahead of us. Sergeant Flowers and Constable Mathieson, I want you to find out everything that you can about The Great Storm of 1913, including what cargo each ship was carrying, particularly the two lost ships reputedly sunk in this area. Right, we will meet again tomorrow."

The men dispersed and Susan packed up her laptop and drove to London where she had another scheduled meeting with the Chief Inspector.

Rose and Tom ate their breakfast outside on the patio. It was a lovely summer's morning with a clear, blue sky and a warm, gentle breeze. Spreading butter thickly on his toast, Tom reached out for Rose's homemade orange marmalade, saying: "So, what have you got on today, love?"

Rose turned to her husband, her green eyes sparkling in the sun and her blonde hair shining with health. Her mind was still replaying the intimate evening that Tom and she had spent following a relaxing soak in the hot tub with a bottle of wine.

"I've put on a casserole to take around to June. While it's

cooking, I've got some research to do. What about you, darling? What are your plans?"

"I'm going to visit mom at Huronview. It's been almost a week since we were last over and I feel a bit guilty."

"Oh, Tom, I would go with you, but I must see June. Give her my love."

Tom's mother had been living at Huronview Nursing Home since her husband, Alan, Tom's father, had died of prostate cancer two years previously. Maureen, his mother, was very alert in her mind, but her legs had given out on her and she was unable to live on her own anymore.

At 90, she was the epitome of the archetypal little old lady with her grey, curly hair and round, rosy cheeks which dimpled when she smiled. Nothing seemed to upset her equilibrium. 'Happy Maureen' they called her at the nursing home.

Whereas many of the elderly sat in chairs looking vacantly out at the world, Maureen wheeled herself into the recreation room and joined in with everything they had going.

Today it was 'Music Appreciation', and when Tom arrived, he found ten elders sitting in the recreation room listening to Vivaldi's Four Seasons. He paused at the doorway to hear the music. It seemed a shame to disturb his mother when she was so clearly enjoying herself. Maureen's eyes lit up when she saw her son Tom standing by the door.

She wheeled her chair out of the room and he followed her to the guest lounge. One of the things Tom and Rose had really liked about Huronview when they had visited was the garden. The courtyard was so pretty, with a stone pathway weaving through pergolas dotted with roses and tubs of geraniums. The sitting room overlooked the garden. Maureen and Tom sat next to the window.

"How's Rose doing? Is she still researching the Great

Storm? Did I tell you that I remember my parents quite clearly telling us all about the storm? My father lost his best friend on The Argus. It certainly was the storm of the century!"

"Yes, well, Rose has spent most of the summer researching the shipwrecks. The Historical Society is putting together a map of where the ships went down with a little biography about each ship and which passengers were aboard. She's pretty well finished it, but now we've been thrown a curve ball by the murder in Bayfield. Rose thinks that the two are connected. She's convinced that it's all to do with one of the shipwrecks."

"She might be onto something there. I remember when they found the Wexford, divers had been searching for years. When was it, 1985, when they finally found it?"

"I think that you mean 2000 that it was found, Mom, unless you're thinking about another boat?"

Tom's mom paused for a minute before saying. "I'm sure that one boat was found in 1985. Maybe you're right, and it probably was 2000. Anyhow, what have you been up to?"

"Not a lot. Rose and I went for a sail yesterday but the wind turned and so we had to head into Grand Bend before returning home. Did you hear about the explosion? Jeff Sinclair, a golfing buddy of mine, was blown up in his boat. It's really quite shocking."

Maureen looked thoughtful. "Sinclair, I think that I know the Sinclair's. Well, not Jeff, but his parents, Ray and Doreen. They've passed on now, but I seem to recall that Jeff took over the family business. They were in the insurance business, dealing mostly with shipping. The business had been in the family for several generations. I believe they were an offshoot of Lloyd's of London. You know, talking of the Great Storm, I do remember my parents saying that there were major claims made by the ships lost and that the insurance companies would have to have paid out a bundle."

"No more talk of boats, Mom. Rose sends her love, and she asks if there is any shopping that you need done."

"She is a dear. No, thanks, I think I'm fine. So, how are my adorable great-grandchildren? Next time you visit you must bring them with you."

"Mom, you know that I can come and pick you up and take you back to Bayfield anytime. Just say when you're feeling up to it."

"But darling, you do appreciate that I'm not very mobile. I don't want to be hoisted into a car and then pulled out and put into a wheelchair. Besides, you don't have the special washrooms that we have here. No Tom, I'm happy enough here. Just bring those little loves, Abby and Ella, over to visit me. That's all that I ask of you."

Tom could understand his mother, as their home wasn't particularly wheelchair accessible and they most certainly did not have a washroom that could accommodate her special needs. *Old age was such a bugger*, he thought as he wrapped his arms around his mom and gave her a big kiss.

"See you soon, Mom. Next time I'll bring Rose and the children."

NINE

W hile Tom had been visiting his mother, Rose had been on the internet trying to track down the details of what cargo each ship was carrying at the time of The Great Storm.

She was able to find the ship's manifest for most of the ships lost and since located, but was having trouble finding the remaining two for the Carruthers and the Hydrus.

At 11:30a.m. she took the casserole out of the oven. It had been slowly cooking for a couple of hours and had infused the kitchen with delicious smells of garlic and onion. Rose left it to cool down on the countertop while she took Ben for a quick walk. This time, instead of going down Mara Street and to the beach, she walked Ben down to Tuyl Street and then on to Delevan and Catherine.

When she passed the Village Book Store, she waved at Mary, the shop owner, and continued on her way. After she filled up Ben's bowl with water, Rose quickly brushed her hair and put on some lipstick. Placing the casserole carefully into the basket on the front of her bicycle, Rose proceeded to peddle over to Victoria Street.

She knocked on June's front door. On the third knock it was opened by a very haggard looking June who appeared to have aged visibly in the week since she had last been at Fitness class. *Grief can eat at the soul and ravage the body with sorrow,* Rose thought as she stood looking at June.

"Oh, June, I'm so, so sorry. I cannot even begin to imagine what you must be going through. Look, I've made you a casserole. I doubt very much if you feel either like cooking or, for that matter, eating?"

"Rose, that's very kind of you. Everyone's been so caring. I honestly just feel overwhelmed."

Rose went over to June and held her in her arms. Glimpsing over her shoulder into the kitchen, she could see at least half a dozen other casserole dishes just like her own. The neighbours had all rallied around.

"Are your daughters here yet?"

"Yes, they've made an appointment to see the Funeral Director in Goderich. The only trouble is the police won't release the body until the pathologists are finished investigating. Oh, Rose, I believe that Jeff was blown to pieces. I just cannot bear the thought of his body being scattered about the place."

Rose looked appalled, but quickly tried to mask her feelings.

"June, you mustn't think about that and, if it's any consolation, Jeff would have died instantly, so he wouldn't have suffered. Please don't dwell on the explosion anymore."

It's easy for me to say that, Rose thought, but if it had been her Tom, she would have felt just the same as June.

"But Jeff was always so careful. Ever since he started

diving for those ships, everything changed. If only we had never met the men from *Diva Diving School.*"

"June, do you know what ships they were interested in? You see, I've been doing some of my own research on the Great Storm of 1913 and discovered that two of the thirteen ships that went down in the storm have never been found. I can't seem to find the manifest for the two ships still missing."

"Oh, Jeff had a list alright. I don't know where it is, but I do know that the cargo aboard one of the ships that he was interested in belonged to a very wealthy family called Stewart-Barclay from Kincardine. I believe that Jeff said that the family had relatives in Bayfield who used to live in a big house in Jewett's Grove. That's all I know. Jeff was rather vague about it all. What he did say was that, if he found the ship and its cargo, his family's name would be somehow vindicated. You know that the family business in Kincardine was almost destroyed by The Great Storm of 1913 because of the insurance claims. Apparently his family was part of the Lloyds syndicate that insured several of the ships lost in the Great Storm and had to pay out huge amounts of money to the owners of the lost ships."

Rose thought about what June had said and something about the name Stewart-Barclay rang a bell. She was almost certain that she had come across that name in the archives somewhere.

She got up to leave.

"June, if there is anything I can do, anything, please don't hesitate to ask. Let me know if you need somewhere for your relatives to stay the day of the funeral. We have two spare bedrooms at your disposal."

Rose hugged June again and left her house feeling so inadequate.

Words seemed so useless at times like this. As long as June didn't feel alone, she would get through it all, but the long, lonely months ahead after the funeral would be when she would most need the support and love of her family and friends.

Stopping off at the archives building, Rose started to open the filing cabinet and, looking at the alphabetically filed index cards, she flicked to the 'S' section. There were several 'Stewarts', but no 'Stewart-Barclay's'.

Maybe it was filed under 'B', for Barclay, Rose thought as she flicked back up to the 'B's'. No, still no Stewart-Barclays.

Rose was about to call it a day when she spied a cardboard box pushed up on the top shelf at the back of the room. The box contained an assortment of photographs and letters and albums from the Brown's attic.

When Alice's mother, Isobel Brown, passed away and before they sold the old house on Catherine Street, Alice had sorted out a box of assorted things she thought the Historical Society might find interesting. Rose had glanced through it, and she now remembered a letter addressed to Mr. R. Stewart-Barclay Esq. Sure enough, almost at the bottom of the box was a brown envelope. It was addressed to Stewart-Barclay of Linwood House, Princess Street, Kincardine.

What it was doing amongst Isobel's memorabilia was beyond Rose.

She opened the envelope and eagerly scanned the contents. Inside was what looked like a ledger sheet written in the most beautiful copperplate writing in sepia toned ink.

It was a manifest for a container load of household contents being shipped by the Hydrus leaving Kincardine on November 8th heading for Point Edward and then on through the St. Clair River, into St. Clair Lake, down to Amherst, and

Windsor, into the Detroit River and Lake Erie, then through the Welland Canal to Lake Ontario, and finally down the St. Lawrance Seaway and across the Atlantic to Rotterdam its final destination. Rose scanned the list of contents and her eyes grew wide as she read the neatly written words.

The Stewart-Barclays were certainly very rich as there were silver candelabras, silver tea sets, and dinner services, Chippendale furniture, some Impressionist paintings, and bottles of wine. The whole container load had been insured for $50,000, which by present-day standards would be the equivalent of at least one million dollars.

But just who were these Stewart-Barclays? Maybe Alice would be able to shed some light on them. Rose played Bridge with Alice every Thursday. She would ask her then. In the meantime, she would Google the name and see what came up. Rose went on to the computer and Googled R. Stewart-Barclay, Kincardine, Ontario, 1913 and to her utter amazement, a whole page of facts about R. Stewart-Barclay came before her on the computer screen.

Without reading the text, Rose printed it off and, looking at her watch, grabbed her bag and left the archives in a rush. Tom would be home and would probably be wondering where she was.

TEN

Her meeting with the Chief hadn't been great. He had wanted to see results and wasn't particularly pleased with the little progress that they had made.

"You know Susan, your case is going cold on you. If you're not careful it's going to die and you'll be left with egg on your face. Have you conducted a house-to-house enquiry?"

"Yes, but Bayfield is such a transient population, cottagers come and go. I'll send the team out again, but right now we're waiting to hear whether it's a case of one or two murders that we're dealing with and that might take some time for forensics and the pathologists to come to a consensus. My instincts tell me that the explosion on the boat was no accident and as the deceased was seen with the two other men, the murdered man and his business partner, it all has to be connected. We're getting close to understanding the motivation. It appears that at least one of the ships that went down in the Great Storm of 1913 contained a very valuable cargo, which we think the divers from *Diva Diving* were planning to retrieve. What happened to cause the murder we have yet to discover and, of course, we just don't, as yet, have a suspect."

The meeting with the Chief Inspector concluded earlier than Susan had expected. She didn't want to go back to Bayfield straight away and so she decided to stop off at Mason-Ville Mall and indulge in some shopping.

Returning to Bayfield later that afternoon, she opened the front door of the cottage and suddenly the sense of loneliness that she had been dreading totally enveloped her and Susan crumpled onto the bed and broke down.

Her relationship with Jim seemed so futile. In fact, her whole life seemed without purpose and aim. She wallowed in her own self-pity for a good hour and then shook her head, washed her tear-stained face, put on some lipstick, retrieved her suitcase from under the bed, and proceeded to pack up her clothes and toiletries.

She would not, and could not, stay in their love-nest any longer. She needed to finish the affair and move on with her life. Enough was enough.

Susan checked into The Bayfield Village Inn. She had stayed there before and loved the indoor swimming pool. She would swim her problems away.

ELEVEN

The next morning, life seemed less bleak.

Moving out of The Cottage Colony had been a good and positive move, and Susan viewed it as the next chapter in her sorry life. For now, she would forget about Jim and concentrate wholly on the murder case.

The team was all assembled when she walked into the room. Their chatting stopped, and all eyes turned to look at their boss. Susan had gone to the hairdressers in Mason Ville and had a change of hair colour. She now sported a platinum blonde Annie Lennox, hair style which made her look stunning.

"Right now, listen up. The Chief is not happy with our progress. He wants us to step up the enquiries. Sergeant Flowers, have you anything to report?"

Sergeant Flowers stood up and proceeded to give the team a mini history lesson on The Great Storm of 1913.

Both Constable Mathieson and he had spent the previous afternoon researching everything they could find on the *Big*

Blow, *The Freshwater Fury*, or *The White Hurricane*, as *The Great Storm* was referred to in various accounts.

As to the two lost ships, they had managed to track down the cargo manifests for three of the ships since found, but the Carruthers and the Hydrus manifests seemed to have disappeared off the face of the earth.

Interestingly, it was both of these ships which had been reported to have sunk off the coast of Port Franks, although The Carruthers could have gone down further north of Goderich. Nobody knew for certain.

He concluded his report and Susan said, "Well, did you go into the archives here in Bayfield? There is a huge amount of research being conducted by a woman called Rose Blair. She would be your best source. How is the house-to-house enquiry going? Give me some good news, please?"

Constable Dailey stood up and, looking down at his notes, he started to read.

"Jeff Sinclair was a local man known and liked by many. The day before his boating incident, he was seen in Brandon's Hardware store where he purchased some heavy-duty nylon rope. He was also seen in Foodland and the LCBO. The only sighting of the three men together was, as already reported, about 3 weeks ago in The Albion bar of the hotel. He appeared to be having a pint with the deceased, Ian, and the missing man, Sam Pierce. That's all I have to report, ma'am."

Susan let out a sigh of exasperation and she fairly snapped back; "That's not good enough. What about in Grand Bend and Port Franks? These men cannot have been invisible?"

Sergeant Flowers stood up. "Well, we have at least tracked the movements of all three men the evening before the murder, and Jeff Sinclair cannot have been with the other two men on the Saturday night. His wife said that he was out drinking with his mates and we checked that out. He was with," he checked his notes, "Ron Smith, Bill White, and Ted Johnson at The Albion until 11:00 p.m. That was confirmed by the barman."

Susan was thoughtful. "Well, that's something positive to go on. We now know that we definitely have a fourth man involved in this case. We can at least rule Jeff Sinclair out of the murder investigation. So, gentlemen, we have two men to find, Sam Pierce and the mystery man. Sergeant Flowers, I want you to concentrate your enquiries on Sam Pierce. Spread your search from here to Lion's Head. Speak to his girlfriend again. Someone somewhere knows something about Sam and we need to know more. Right, get to it, team. Our next briefing will be at the same time tomorrow."

The team dispersed and Susan sat there, deep in thought. Solving any case was like putting together a giant jigsaw puzzle. Right now they seemed to have all the border, straight edge pieces in place, but there were still an awful lot of gaps still left in the middle to piece together.

Rose arrived home just as Tom was pulling into the drive-way. He got out of the car and went over to her and gave her a big kiss.

"Mom sends her love. How did it go with your visit to June?"

"Oh, Tom, it's so awful. She's being so brave, but is clearly devastated. Anyway, it looks like the neighbours have all dropped off food. I think that my casserole was about the sixth one, but she can always freeze them. I dropped by the archives, and you'll never guess what I found - the cargo manifest for the Hydrus. There was a container aboard the ship transporting one family's whole household of belongings. They must have been quite wealthy. The Insurance was valued at fifty thousand dollars, which by today's standards would be more like one million dollars."

"Go on, who were these wealthy people? I can see that you're just dying to tell me!"

"Come inside first. I'll make us a nice cup of tea and tell you,"

Rose said as she lifted her bag out of her bicycle basket and headed for the front door with Tom close on her heels.

Inside, it was lovely and cool. The August temperatures were still up in the 90s and although both Tom and Rose adored the summer heat, having a lovely cool house was a positive joy. Rose put the kettle on and Tom got out the mugs. When the tea was made, Rose grabbed her bag and, with a hot, steaming mug of tea in hand, she walked out to the sun lounge followed by the ever-faithful Ben and Tom. Tom plonked himself down on the comfy sofa and Rose took one of the armchairs and Ben another.

"Right, come on, show me what you've got, you're being very mysterious."

Rose smiled and pulled out the brown envelope containing the cargo manifest.

"I think that I know why that man was murdered, Tom. I suspect it has to do with them searching for this ship containing millions of dollars' worth of cargo. Look, the container was insured through Sinclair and Sons of Kincardine. The contents were owned by a Mr. R. Stewart-Barclay of Kincardine. Just read this and look at the lovely copperplate writing. Isn't it neat?"

"Rose darling, where on earth did you get this from?"

"Oh, it was in a box of memorabilia from Alice Bradbury's mother, Isobel Brown's house. There were mostly photographs and old postcards and some letters. This was buried right at the bottom. I haven't a clue why a ship's manifest should find its way into Isobel Brown's house in the first place."

"Well, you've certainly discovered something here. You know that you'll have to pass all of this on to the police. It could be very important to them."

"I made a photocopy of the ledger, but I did think that I would pop over to the Lion's Hall tomorrow morning and hand this over to Susan. I wanted to see her again and maybe invite her over for a barbecue this weekend. But first, I want to study this print out I got from Googling this R. Stewart-Barclay. By the way, the 'R' stands for Richard and from what I can see this Richard had a very colourful life."

Rose started to read aloud what really amounted to a mini biography of Richard Stewart-Barclay.

"He was born in Reading, Berkshire, England, in 1867 to a wealthy landowning family. The Barclays were cousins of the famous Barclay bankers, but they were old money dating back to Richard III. Richard was the second son and therefore, not destined to inherit the family estate. He made his mark in the first Anglo-Zulu war where, in 1879, he was one of eleven recipients to receive the Victoria Cross for bravery after rescuing his Captain at Rourke's Drift. After the Boer war, he returned to England where he almost immediately set sail for Canada. He made his name in Petrolia, where oil had been discovered twenty years prior. He purchased a piece of land from a William McGarvey and had a great gusher, which made him a millionaire almost overnight. He and William McGarvey became good friends. William and his wife, Helena, introduced Richard to Helena's niece, Sophia. Richard and Sophia married and lived in Petrolia for 8 years getting to know all the oil barons; Fairbanks, King and Jake Englehart. Sophia and Charlotte Englehart became great friends. Neither woman ever managed to have children."

Rose paused her reading and thought about the one and only time that she had visited the town of Petrolia. It was a small town with a big history. In its day, Petrolia carried the heaviest tax base in the whole of Canada! It could have developed into something akin to Dallas, had oil not been discovered in Pennsylvania. The beautiful oil barons' houses lay testimony to the wealth of the town in years gone by. She returned to reading Richard Stewart's biography.

"In 1901, Richard and Sophia left Petrolia to set up home in Kincardine, where Sophia's sister lived. They built themselves a grand mansion on Princess Street, Linwood House, and became local philanthropists. In 1913, Richard received a letter from William McGarvey, his old friend who had discovered a rich oil field in Galicia, Prussia. He asked Richard if he would join him in the venture with equal shares. Richard and Sophia decided to travel to Prussia to join the McGarvey's, whose daughter had just married Count Von Zeppelin that year. They booked their passage aboard a ship leaving from Montreal to Rotterdam and sent their container load of household belongings on a cargo ship, the Hydrus, which left Kincardine on November 8th, 1913.

By the time the Stewart-Barclays arrived in Prussia, it was the summer of 1914. They had stopped off in England to visit Richard's family in Berkshire and their stay had been extended due to Richard's father's ailing health. They finally arrived in Galicia the same month that Franz Joseph and his wife were assassinated. War was declared.

Richard and Sophia were killed when a bomb exploded on the train that they were travelling on just outside of Düsseldorf on September 5th, 1914.

William McGarvey spent the following two years of the war rescuing his fellow Canadian oil drillers, whom he had brought over to work in his oil fields. He died in 1915, a broken man.

The Stewart-Barclays never heard about the storm that sank the ship carrying their cargo. Sophia's sister in Kincardine was one of the few people who were aware of the sheer value of the cargo. The only other people privy to this were the insurance brokers and shipping agents, Sinclair and Son's."

"Wow, what a story!" Tom said when they had finished reading. "So Jeff must have known about this ledger, or why else would he be involved with the others in diving for the Hydrus?"

"Well, Jeff worked for his father years ago, but when they moved to Bayfield, he pretty well retired from mainstream underwriting. He just kept a few of his old clients on his books. He may not have known about the full extent of the manifest unless he was deliberately looking. After all, this was all one hundred years ago and why would he wait so long to look for the lost ships if he knew about them years ago?"

"I'm not sure, but what I do know is that we must pass all of this on to Susan. Right now though, what do you want for dinner tonight?"

Susan went to The Albion for dinner. She couldn't face going to The Black Dog or The Docks, as they were places that she associated with Jim. She sat outside on the veranda in front of the pub and ordered a hamburger and fries plus a large gin and tonic. The place was positively heaving with people and she could see that The Black Dog was equally busy. The following Saturday would be the Bayfield Fall Fair and then it would be countdown for the end of the summer.

If they hadn't solved the murder by Labour Day weekend,

Susan had decided that they would move the incident room to London. She had also decided that she would not be meeting up with Jim again in Bayfield. If he came to her condo in London, she would formally end their relationship then and there. Already, with her mind made up, she was steeling herself for Jim's phone call. He normally phoned her at least two or three times a week.

Back at the Bayfield Village Inn, Susan decided to take her frustrations out in the pool.

Swimming had always been therapeutic to her, and today was no exception. Susan swam fifty lengths doing a steady crawl, only stopping twice for a small break. Her condo had a swimming pool in the basement for the use of the residents. She tried to swim at least three times a week. It kept her fit both in body and in mind.

After her swim, Susan went to her room, watched some television, and went to bed at 9:00 p.m. She fell asleep instantly. Swimming always did that to her, made her sleep like a baby.

TWELVE

Thursday was her day for Bridge. Rose liked the social aspect of the game, but didn't like the competition. There were normally at least five tables of four set up. Today, because the Lion's Hall was being used for the Police Inquiry, they were meeting at The Bayfield Town Hall. Rose had offered to make a coffee cake for the after-game refreshments. She hoped that Alice Bradbury was going to be there.

The Town Hall was such a thriving place. When Rose and Tom had first moved to the village, they had thought that it was a church. It did, indeed, look like a church with its white clapboard and its bell tower and steep pitched roof. Concerts, plays, weddings, parties, yoga, Tai Chi, and any number of meetings took place in the old building which had been a town hall in 1882 and even sported a jail. Nowadays, the jail was used as a storeroom.

There was an active group of people in the 1980s who fought hard to save the town hall when the municipality threatened to demolish the building. A town hall committee now met once a month to keep the place alive. Rose hoped to join the committee one day and had indeed been asked to consider a position on the Board in the New Year.

The Bridge game began. Rose was partnered with Sara Wandsworth, who lived out of the village on Pavilion Road. They were to play Duplicate Bridge and Sara would remain her partner for the duration of the game. Sara was a much better Bridge player than Rose. After each round was completed, the two of them would move to the next table and play against another team until all five rounds had been played.

Finally, the last game was played and Rose was able to look around to see if her friend Alice was also finished. She was.

Rose went over to her and said, "Alice, you know that box full of photos and old postcards that you donated to The Historical Society? Well, I found an interesting invoice, well, really, a ledger account addressed to a Mr. R. Stewart-Barclay. Have you any idea why your parents would have this in their procession?"

Alice was about to bite into a large slice of the coffee cake Rose had made. She hesitated, put the cake back on her plate, and looked at Rose.

"Well, Mother and Father were related to the Stewart-Barclays of Kincardine. I think that his wife, I believe that her name was Sophia, was my grandma's distant cousin or something like that.

My grandparents lived in Kincardine for a short time, before my mother was born. You know, Rose, I think that there was some scandal attached to the Stewart-Barclays. My mother would never talk about it, but my grandmother was a huge snob. She used to talk about the nouveau riche and considered anyone who was a self-made man vulgar. I do know that the Stewart-Barclays left their mark on Kincardine in more than one way. Did you know that they were one of the founders of the Kincardine Hospital?

Alice looked thoughtful as she paused to take another bite of her piece of cake. "Mrs. Stewart-Barclay was quite involved in the whole process. They were quite the philanthropists, people with lots of money quite often were in those days. You should talk to my son, John. He did his PhD thesis based on the social history of Kincardine. Actually, I gave him that box of photos and stuff to look through before sending it to The Historical Society. John and his family are coming down from Cambridge for a few days tomorrow. If you and Tom would like to pop over for a drink, I'm sure that John could fill you in on the history of Kincardine."

"Wow, thank you, Alice. Great, Tom and I will be there. What time would be good for you?"

"How about four o'clock? Dave and I have a game of Croquet to play in the morning and I'm sure that John, Lucy, and the kids will be on the beach all day but by 4.00 p.m. they will be more than ready to partake in a drink or two."

"We'll bring a bottle of wine and I'll make some appetizers. I look forward to chatting with John."

Rose left the Town Hall and cycled back home. She could hardly wait to meet John and to find out more about the Stewart-Barclays.

Susan greeted the team with greater enthusiasm than before. She had slept so well after her lengthy swim and, in doing so, had managed to put the case clearly into perspective. Thinking everything through, she realized that in the nine days they had uncovered quite a serious amount of mileage.

They now knew, and had tracked down, the last day of Ian Richard's life, had established the motivation behind the men's visit to Bayfield, knew that four people were involved, and that Jeff Sinclair could not be the murderer but he was somehow involved in the case.

She hoped that Sergeant Flowers and Mathieson might shed further light on the investigation.

"Right, let's have some good news. Sergeant Flowers, what have you got for us?"

The Sergeant stood up and pulled out his notebook.

"I showed these three photographs of Ian, Sam, and Jeff extensively from here to Lion's Head. In Wingham, I talked to a girl behind the counter at Tim Hortons and she thought that she had seen the three men sitting at a table with another man who also seemed familiar. This was about 3 weeks ago. In Lion's Head, Ian and Sam were recognized by many people and in the pub down by the marina, the waitress recognized the photograph of Jeff and once again claimed that there was a fourth man in the group. That was back in June. I met with Sam's girlfriend and she was pretty cut up. They were a close couple, and she definitely felt that Sam would not have purposely avoided contacting her. She hasn't heard from him for ten days now. She did say that before he left for Bayfield, he was pretty pumped up about something. He never mentioned anything about shipwrecks, but he did say that 'J' was planning a big dive. She did not know who 'J' was, but Sam apparently often referred to people by the first letter of their name. Ian and Sam were good friends, as well as successful business partners. That concludes my report."

"Constable Dailey, anything to report?"

"Well, I went to the Bayfield Archives, and the archivist told me that Mrs. Rose Blair would be in tomorrow. While I was there, I had a look around and opened the filing cabinet to check who was who in and around Bayfield in the early 1900s. I also looked up what the ships were transporting up and down the lake one hundred years ago. Grain seemed to be the biggest export, grain, and wood. Places like Kincardine, which, by the way, was then called Penetangore, were pretty isolated and could only be reached by water until The Wellington Grey Bruce railway was opened in 1874."

Constable Dailey started to pace up and down as he warmed to his brief history of the area circa 1880. "The road from Durham and Guelph was cut through the dense forests in 1857, but it was very rough and almost impassable in the winter. In the early 1900s, R. C. Coombe and Watson opened a huge furniture factory in Kincardine. It was so successful that furniture was exported all over the world by cargo ships. During the Great Storm of 1913 at least one cargo ship was carrying furniture from Coombe and Watson's furniture factory."

The Constable referred to his notebook again and continued with his lecture. "Many of the ships were insured with Sinclair and Sons of Kincardine. I checked to see who the owners of the company actually were. Well, really, how many sons there were involved in the business. The original owner was Hugh Sinclair and his three sons, Luke, John, and James, who worked for their father. After the Great Storm, the company suffered huge losses and old Hugh died the following year. Luke and John continued to run the insurance business, but they no longer insured sailing vessels. James went off on his own and set up his own business. Our Jeff Sinclair was born to Luke and Harriet Sinclair in 1947. Luke had survived the Second World War, but his brother, John, was killed in France. James married Maria and they had two daughters,

Mary and Denise. In 1951, Denise gave birth to a boy and Mary had two boys, one in 1952 and the other in 1954. That's about all I've got up to, ma'am. I hope to be able to speak to Mrs. Blair tomorrow."

Susan looked impressed. Her team had come through, and things were beginning to make sense. She thanked them all and wrapped up the meeting. They still had no conclusive report back from forensics, but she was pretty well convinced that the explosion had not been the result of some unfortunate accident.

Tom had been out playing golf while Rose was at bridge. As was often the case, they both arrived back at the same time, Rose on her bicycle and Tom in their Volvo. Immediately they knew that something was wrong, as they could hear Ben barking frantically in the back garden. When they had both left that morning, he was sound asleep in his dog basket in the kitchen. Had someone put him in the garden?

"Rose, did you lock the front door before you left this morning?" Tom asked as he pushed open the unlocked door.

Rose looked guilty. If the truth be told, she had never locked the door since moving to Bayfield.

They both walked into their home, and Rose quickly went to the back door to let Ben in. The poor dog seemed beside himself, but at least he was alive, Rose thought as she walked nervously through the living room.

"It doesn't look as if anything has been stolen, Tom. Look, our television and stereo are still here. In fact, nothing even looks disturbed. How weird!"

"Well, it doesn't make any sense. Why would anyone go to the trouble of breaking in and not take anything?"

Rose was staring at her laptop and all the papers spread

out on the coffee table in the sun lounge. Had she left them like that? She could have sworn that she had put them all back in the green folder. On closer inspection she realized that the brown envelope containing the ships' manifest was missing.

"Oh, Tom, the cargo ledger from the Hydrus is missing. Who would break into our house just to steal that?"

"Well, my love, I'm going to call the police. Do you have Susan's cell number?"

Rose gave it to him and she walked around the room feeling a little sick. It felt like such a violation of their privacy. Just the thought of someone going through her papers made her feel somehow betrayed. Tom came over to her and put his arms around her shoulders.

"Don't worry, love, your friend will be over very soon. She'll get to the bottom of this for us, you just wait and see."

Rose felt infuriatingly like crying. Her eyes watered, and her lips quivered. *What a baby I am*, she thought while clinging to Tom.

True to her word, Susan was at their house within five minutes.

Rose felt slightly embarrassed as there was no evidence of foul play.

Only she knew that the envelope was missing and, of course, Ben had been shut in the garden. She shook her head to clear it and realized that Susan had been talking.

"Whoever put your dog in the garden probably knew him. Who else would risk being attacked by a big black dog?"

"So, you reckon whoever came into our house is someone we know? That creeps me out even more than if it had been a stranger."

"You said that the envelope contained an old ledger of a

cargo ship. What was so important about it that someone would break into your house?"

"Actually, I was going to bring it over to you to read, as I think that it could be relevant to your case. I found it in an old box of photographs and papers donated to The Bayfield Historical Society."

"Just where did you get the box from?"

"My friend Alice found it in her mother's attic when she was clearing everything out to sell the property."

"Why was this manifest so important? You mentioned that it might be relevant to my case?"

Rose explained how she had been researching the cargo aboard the ships lost in The Great Storm of 1913.

She concluded by saying, "I am, of course, making a big assumption when I say that I think that the men involved in the murder were looking for the cargo aboard the Hydrus. It's just that it is such a valuable cargo and one that could be salvaged. The big question is, did they succeed in finding the lost ship and if so, did they find the cargo?"

Susan looked impressed.

"Rose, you should be on our team. You've come to a similar conclusion about the motive driving this case as we have with all of our questioning and heavy leg work. But we are still no closer to fathoming out who the fourth person is and whether Sam Pierce is alive or dead."

"If I were you, I would be looking at who knew about the ship and its cargo. I'm assuming that you know all about Jeff Sinclair's connection to the case through his father's business?"

"I know something about his family, but I feel sure that you're about to enlighten me further."

Rose spent the following thirty minutes telling Susan about the Stewart-Barclays and Sinclair and Sons. When she had finished telling Susan, she realized that there were gaps in her narrative. Hopefully, Alice's son, John, would help her fill in the gaps.

Susan left, but not before she heavily chastised Rose for not locking up the house.

"There are predators out there and they know that people like you have been lulled into a false sense of security."

Rose felt like a schoolgirl being told off by the teacher. She couldn't stop herself from saying:

"Yes, teacher. I'm sorry teacher."

They both laughed and Susan drove away in her big, black, unmarked cruiser. Rose looked at Tom and rolled her eyes.

"I think that I need that gin and tonic."

After she left Rose and Tom's house, Susan went back to The Bayfield Village Inn. It was too early to go out to eat, and she didn't really want to just stay in her bedroom and watch television. That was the trouble with being single; everything was fine during the day when work kept her busy, but the evenings were just so lonely. Susan hated the evenings.

She decided to take a road trip up to Kincardine. All the talk of the Stewart-Barclays had whetted her appetite, and she had never been to the town before, so it would be some place different for her to visit. She changed into more casual clothes and locked her room.

The drive to Kincardine was very pleasant. Late afternoon was always a good time to be on the road in the summer.

Driving up Highway 21 she passed through Goderich, a town so ravaged by the tornado of 2011 nobody could ever have imagined that it would ever look the same. But the Square had been reborn spectacularly; it now looked ten times better than before.

The people of Goderich must have felt so proud because it had truly been a community effort to restore the dignity and presence once more to 'Ontario's Prettiest Town'.

The Highway took her across the Maitland River in one majestic sweep. On the bluff overlooking the river lay Tiger Dunlop's memorial. *Now that was one amazing man*, thought Susan as she drove up the hill and past the sign for the airport.

Huron County was full of interesting characters who'd left their mark in one way or another. Those early pioneers had molded and shaped the area into the thriving county that it had become.

Although Huron was very much considered a rural county, the shore of Lake Huron was dotted with villages and towns that in years gone by had made a living from the lake; fishing, boat building, and then the tourist industry, not forgetting one of the world's biggest salt mines in Goderich.

Kincardine had made its name in the furniture business, and now it was primarily associated with The Bruce Nuclear Power Generating Plant situated just north of the town. Nothing ever stayed the same, Susan reflected. Change was a pivotal part of survival, reinvention and renewal, the mainstay of progress.

The drive took her past Point Farms Conservation Area, which jolted Susan's memory. It had been here that she had been a part of another murder scene, also a lone body found on the beach. She had only been out of the police academy for two years and was a real rookie, but the experience had shaped her. The Chief in charge was Inspector Robson. He had been close to retirement then, and she wondered where he was now.

She had learnt so much from him, particularly how to

listen to your gut or instinct, how to keep the team all on the same page, how to be methodical and to leave no stone unturned. If truth be known, Susan had a mighty crush on the Inspector, a misplaced crush because as it transpired the man was gay. Back in those days the police force was very largely homophobic, which was sad.

She was about to drive past the turn off for Port Albert when Susan remembered that her old friends, Cindy, and Pete, had a cottage close to the beach nearby. On an impulse she swung off the highway, turning left towards the port. She had only been to their cottage once before and that had been at least ten years ago; she hoped that she could still find it. Taking another left turn just before the river, she knew immediately that she was in the right place. The steep and rutted dirt road had been cut into a dense forest.

A hundred years ago the whole of Huron County would have been nothing but trees, but now little cottages nestled almost hidden in the deep foliage.

She found Cindy and Pete's cottage and joy upon joy there was a car parked in front. Jumping out of her car, Susan surveyed the scene. The cottage itself had changed substantially since she had last visited. An extension had been built onto what now looked like a large garage.

A wooden boardwalk connected the two buildings and a large cobble stone fire pit now took centre stage in the garden. She could hear voices and was about to knock on the door when Cindy appeared.

She was a petite, pixie-like woman with thick, curly black hair and a freckled face.

"My God, if it isn't Susan Parker! Pete, look who's come to visit!"

Pete came to the door, opened it wide, and gave Susan a huge bear hug. He was a big, robust man with a large belly but a huge, friendly face.

"Gosh, it's been so long. How are you? Where have you been these past ten years?"

Susan never reached Kincardine. Instead, she spent one of the best evenings that she had experienced in many years. Old friends felt so comfortable, just like an old pair of slippers. They talked late into the night, getting through several bottles of wine. Cindy had insisted that Susan stay over, as there was no way she would be fit to drive. She could drive back to Bayfield early the next morning.

Catching up on old times, remembering little snippets from the past, the two women had a shared history. They both had been at university together. "Oh, and I have to tell you that I bumped into Rose Tredle in Bayfield. She hasn't changed a bit. She's married to a lovely man, Tom Blair, and they have three children. They seem so happy and I'm so jealous."

"Rose, yes, I remember her. You two were quite close. She must have retired from teaching by now?"

"Yes, they've retired and have built the most gorgeous house in Bayfield. Talking of houses, where do you both live?"

"Oh, we moved around a bit because of Pete's work. It made it difficult for me with teaching but now we live in St. Mary's, just north of London, near Stratford. You would know it well enough. Gosh, to think we've been living so close to you all this time and we haven't seen each other for ten years. That's crazy!"

They exchanged email addresses and cell phone numbers and promised to keep in touch.

THIRTEEN

S usan left the following morning feeling warm and happy. *That's what an injection of friendship could do to a bruised soul*, she thought as she drove down the highway.

Stopping at The Red Cat Bakery, she bought a baguette and some bread rolls. The smell of freshly baked bread was enough to make her feel ravenously hungry. She sank her teeth into the warm baguette and devoured the crispy crust and warm, fluffy bread in seconds. *What a way to start the day*, she thought as she drove through Goderich and headed for Bayfield.

There was a general air of expectancy hovering in the Incident Room at the Lion's Hall in Bayfield. Susan loved it when a case started coming together. The buzz created could be felt by everyone, and it was hugely infectious.

"Right. I can see by your faces that things are buzzing. Let's have our first report, Sergeant Flowers, please."

Sergeant Flowers stood up and proceeded to read from his notebook.

"Jeff Sinclair's grandfather started a business in Kincardine as an Underwriter for Lloyd's of London insuring the ships and cargo. There were many of these insured ships lost in The Great Storm of 1913 and this almost bankrupted the firm. There were three sons in the business, two of them continued to run Sinclair and Sons after their father died. The third son branched off on his own in a different direction by starting a haulage business, which became quite successful as the railway and highway networks improved across Canada. His company was based in Wingham."

Sergeant Flowers paused, scratched his nose and continued. "The three lost ships had a combined worth of over two million dollars. The Hydrus alone was valued at close to fifty thousand. According to June Sinclair, her husband, Jeff, was diving for the shipwrecks and, although he never told her, she has surmised that Ian and Sam were also interested in the salvage operation. Sam Pierce's girlfriend found the letter 'J' next to a list of the lost ships. The 'J' could be our Jeff Sinclair. Now I did speak to Mrs. Blair in the archives. She was noticeably upset about a break-in that had occurred in her house. An old ledger account had been stolen. This manifest listed the full contents of the cargo aboard the Hydrus. She had, however, made a photocopy of the documents and I have that with me here."

The Sergeant held up a sheaf of papers, the photocopied ships manifest. "This ship contained a very valuable cargo, a profitable salvage operation for anyone able to find the lost ship. I learnt much about The Great Storm and spent an informative hour in the archives with Mrs. Blair. That concludes my report."

Susan did not have the heart to let on to the Sergeant that

most of what he had reported she had already learnt from Rose the previous afternoon.

"Thank you, Sergeant. Has anyone else got anything to report?"

Constable Dailey stood up and opened a plastic bag. He pulled out a three-foot length of chain.

"This, ma'am, was found on the beach not far from where the body was discovered. It looks very much like our murder weapon."

"Constable, who found this chain?"

"A Mr. Gough. He was walking on the beach yesterday evening when the setting sun glinted off something metal. He was going to toss it when he found that it was only a chain but his wife said that she had heard that the murdered man had been strangled and so he handed it in this morning."

Susan looked pleased.

"Thank you, Constable, good work. Now, we have every-thing in place except for the identity of the murderer and the whereabouts of Sam Pierce. It appears that the motive for this murder is tied up with the valuable cargo aboard the Hydrus. We still have no idea who the fourth man is, but I can now confirm that Jeff Sinclair's boat was definitely sabotaged. Forensics have found traces of nitroglycerin on some of the engine pieces plus the sheer size of the explosion indicates a bomb was used to blow up the boat. We are definitely looking at two murders and one missing man. We need to concentrate on finding this fourth man and Sam Pierce. Right, keep ques-tioning the public and report back tomorrow morning."

The men dispersed, leaving Susan quietly to her thoughts. Somehow the murder was intrinsically tied up with the history of the Great Storm of 1913. Of this she was sure.

Although Tom and Rose had been retired for three years and that meant that weekends and weekdays were no different from each other, they still had kept to their routine of lying in bed on a Saturday morning, having breakfast in bed while reading the Saturday papers.

The Globe and Mail was sprawled open on the bed, the travel section in Rose's hands while Tom read the sports section. Ben lay flat out on the bottom of their bed snoring away gently.

"Tom, do you fancy a holiday? Do you realize we haven't had a proper holiday in three years?"

Tom ignored Rose. He was totally absorbed in what he was reading. She pulled his paper away and repeated her question.

"I gather that you want to go on holiday, love. Any particular destination in mind?"

"Well, I've always wanted to go to Austria. Susan said that she was in Austria with her boyfriend last Spring and she said that it has to be the most romantic city in the world. She told me that there were streets filled with intimate cafes. I think she mentioned one street called Kaartnstrasse. You know something, she let it slip that Jim Reynolds, the guy we saw her with at The Docks? Well she said that Jim goes to Vienna regularly and has one particular café that he just loves on the Kaartnstrasse. Look, there's a whole long article on Vienna and it even mentions Kaartnstrasse and it says that it is one of Vienna's most romantic streets. Air Canada has some great offers if you book before October."

Tom reluctantly put his paper down and read the travel section. He had to admit that Vienna looked amazing and the price for two weeks in Austria staying in a castle no less was a great deal. "Well, we'll do it. How about next month in three weeks' time?"

"How exciting! It's years since we've been to Europe. "

Rose hugged her husband, sending all the papers flying and waking up poor Ben with a start.

"So, what have we got on today after I've booked this trip?" Tom asked as he picked up the newspapers and started to sort out the sports section again.

"This afternoon we're going over to Alice and Dave's house for drinks. That reminds me, I promised to bring around some appetizers. I think that you've played golf with Dave before and Alice is one of my bridge buddies but it's actually their son, John, whom I want to talk to. He's up with his family for the weekend, and I want to pick his brain about the history of Kincardine. We're to be there at around four this afternoon."

"Well, that's good because I wanted to spend awhile working on the boat. I'll go down to the marina after breakfast. Speaking of breakfast, I'm cooking. Bacon and eggs for you, my love?"

Tom enjoyed cooking breakfast. It was the one meal that Rose disliked making. Traditionally, they always had a cooked breakfast over the weekends.

"Just give me twenty minutes to shower and wash my hair," Rose said as she got out of bed and padded to the bathroom.

The day had begun.

Susan decided to check out the Harbour Lights Marina. Maybe someone might recognize the photographs of Ian, Sam, and Jeff. She knew that Sergeant Flowers and Mathieson had asked around the South Shore Marina where Jeff Sinclair had kept his boat, but as far as she knew they had not extended their enquiries to the main Harbour Lights Marina.

Parking her car down by the side of The Cottage Colony was more out of habit than anything else. Susan caught herself holding her breath as she looked at the cabin Jim and she had shared and made passionate love in - their love nest. She had rehearsed in her mind all the things she would say to Jim when he telephoned, but he had not phoned her and that was unusual. Over the past year, he had been particularly good at keeping in touch.

Maybe, thought Susan, *just maybe he has decided to call it quits, too.* Irrationally, this thought bothered her but she let it go. She could see Tom standing on a lovely, white sailboat with the name *Tranquillity* painted on the side. *A perfect name for a perfect couple*, Susan thought as she walked towards Tom. *I could really fancy him* was another fleeting thought as she reached the boat and called out, 'Hi!' Tom had been so absorbed in waxing the boat deck, he hadn't heard her approach.

"Oh Susan, fancy seeing you here! Can I help you with anything?"

"No, Tom, I'm just down here showing photographs to anyone I can see. Not many people about today? I thought that on a beautiful sunny morning like this it would be teeming with people."

Tom looked at her and said, "No breeze. Sail boats need wind and today, so far, the lake is as calm as a mill pond."

Susan's eyes scanned the row of boats tied up in their slips. A few motor cruisers were gliding out of the harbour and into the lake; some were probably fishermen, although the expense of owning one of the slick cruisers belied the idea of them being used as fishing boats. Susan looked over to where Jim kept his boat. The slip was empty, his boat gone. With a jolt, Susan realized that Jim must be in town. Why hadn't he called her? Walking back to Tom, Susan casually pointed to Jim's empty slip.

"Tom, did you see a boat leave from this slip? My friend Jim keeps his boat here and I wonder if you noticed it leaving?"

Tom straightened his back and looked over towards the empty slip.

"There was a boat leaving the dock just as I arrived at about ten this morning. It could have been his boat."

Susan nodded and pulled out her cell phone. She checked to see that it was on and then scrolled down to see if there were any messages, but there were none from Jim. She turned to say goodbye to Tom and missed her footing, twisting her ankle awkwardly.

"Ouch...ow, that hurts." She cried out, and Tom jumped off the boat and helped her to hobble over to one of the benches nearby.

He was amazed at the lightness of her body as he pulled her up and put his arms around her shoulders to support her as she walked. *She felt lithe and sinewy, like a cat,* he thought as he leaned down to examine her ankle which had already started to swell and bruise.

Susan rubbed her ankle and moaned softly.

"What a darn fool I am, a clumsy one at that. Thank you for helping me. Do you think I need to go to the hospital?"

Tom looked again at her ankle and couldn't stop himself from admiring her shapely legs, but of course he did not say anything other than, "No, the ankle isn't broken, just sprained. You might have to rest up for a day or two and it will probably swell up some more, but you'll be ok. I'm sure that you don't want to spend the day in the emergency room. Try to stand up, hold on to my shoulder and see if you can put any pressure on it."

Susan stood and gingerly put her foot on the ground. It was excruciatingly painful, but she could just about hobble towards her car.

"Thank God that it's my left foot and not my right, otherwise I wouldn't be able to drive."

Susan hung onto Tom until they reached her car. She liked the feeling of closeness she got from being next to him. Without thinking, she turned to him and kissed him. For a few seconds, Tom looked deeply into her sorrowful eyes.

He could drown in those eyes, and he felt himself falling and at the same time being aroused in a way he hadn't felt for years. His breath came in short gasps as he pulled away from Susan and then he took her lovely head in his hands and, running his fingers through her hair, he kissed her again, this time a long, lingering coupling of their lips. He felt her hot body melt into his as time stood still. Suddenly Tom pulled away and held her at arm's length.

"This is neither the time nor place," Tom said. "Much as I'm very attracted to you, I also happen to love my wife who is also my best friend. This isn't a good idea."

Susan looked at him and quickly said, "You're a good man, Tom. Rose is lucky to have you."

Rose was busy making fig and goat cheese tarts when Tom returned home. He seemed rather quiet and disappeared off to the study as soon as he got in. It was three o'clock and there would still be time to take Ben for a walk before getting ready to go to Alice and Dave's.

"Tom, do you want to come with me to take Ben for a walk?"

Rose called as she clipped the leash on Ben's collar.

"No, thank you, I've got some work to do here, I'll see you later." When Tom talked about work, he usually meant paying bills.

He did everything online and was normally very efficient at keeping up to date with the household accounts.

Ben, as usual, dictated their walk generally by smells that he couldn't resist following. This time his nose took him to Louisa Street and once again Rose mused about the history of Bayfield and how a hundred years ago Louisa had actually been the Main thoroughfare through the village. The Geimenharts had owned apple orchards along the street with which they made cider and schnapps, although the family was primarily known for its furniture making.

Ben and Rose walked the length of Louisa Street to Clan Gregor Square; they then walked down Main Street past the Albion which Rose could never pass without thinking of the tragic events that had haunted the old hotel. A ghost was reputed to squeak the boards, probably the ghost of young Harvey Elliott who was murdered in cold blood by his own brother, Fred. That poor mother, Mrs. Elliott, who had herself lost a son and her husband in short succession, and then she had to deal with the murder of another son. *Poor woman*, Rose thought for the hundredth time.

Ben turned down Charles Street past Maud Stirling and her sister's house to Colina Street, where they turned left and ended up back on Bayfield Terrace. They arrived home just after 3:30p.m. Tom was still in the study, so Rose went to their bedroom and changed into a lovely, fresh yellow cotton sundress. She brushed her hair and put on some lipstick.

Going back to the kitchen, Rose arranged the tarts on to a pottery platter and covered it all with some plastic wrap.

"Tom, we're leaving in ten minutes. Are you ready?"

Tom appeared shortly afterwards. He had changed into a pale blue short-sleeved shirt which matched his eyes beautifully and had taken his grubby shorts off and replaced them with a crisp pair of khaki pants. He still seemed subdued and kept averting his eyes from Rose.

"Are you feeling alright, my love?" Rose asked, genuinely worried about the strange behaviour Tom was exhibiting.

"Look, we don't have to go. If you don't feel like it, I could give Alice a call. She'd understand."

"No, I'm fine, Rose. Just a bit tired. Let's go."

They drove over to Tuyl Street in silence. Alice and Dave's house overlooked the lake and although the house itself wasn't anything special, the setting and garden were spectacular. The back lawn was manicured immaculately and sloped in terraces down to a wooden deck. This was cantilevered out to form a viewing platform which overlooked Lake Huron and its amazing sunsets.

Rose introduced Tom to everyone and Alice beckoned to her son, John, to come and meet Rose.

John was forty-four and a very good-looking man at that. He was tall and athletic, with the kind of loose limbs associated with marathon runners. There was, however, an arrogance about the man that instantly rankled Rose.

"I understand that you want me to fill you in on the history of Kincardine. You might have to camp out here if I really get going."

"Well, a condensed version would be good. I'm really

looking for information about a Mr. Stewart-Barclay and his wife."

John looked thoughtful.

"This wouldn't by any chance have anything to do with the old ledger in that box full of old photos and postcards that my mother gave to The Historical Society?"

"Well, partially, although I was researching The Great Storm of 1913 and it was then that I found out about the Stewart-Barclays. What can you tell me about them?"

"Well let me see. The Stewart-Barclays arrived on the scene in Kincardine around 1901. Sophia, Stewart-Barclay's wife, had relatives, I think a sister, living in the town. Her husband, Richard, had made his fortune in Petrolia in Lambton County during the oil boom. They moved to Kincardine and built a huge mansion on Princess Street. Sophia became a very good friend of Madam Josephine Gualco who was the wife of Francisco Gualco an Italian migrant from Montreal. Alexander Mackenzie and Francisco became partners and made an absolute fortune in Brazil setting up utilities in Sao Paulo and Rio de Janeiro. Mr. and Mrs. Gualco travelled extensively throughout Europe and Brazil but always called Kincardine home. In 1909, after her husband's death, Madam Gualco bought the Queen Street North Grant property and donated it for the creation of a hospital."

John stopped and looked thoughtful as he fidgeted with his pen. He continued his lecture with an almost monotone voice. "She also left an annual endowment of $2500 for the running of the hospital. Sophia, Richard Stewart-Barclay's wife, helped Josephine with the plans for the hospital. Ironically, later that same year, in December 1908, Sophie's other good friend from Petrolia, Charlotte Englehart, on her death bequeathed in her will her own home and an annual endowment fund to estab-

lish a hospital in Petrolia where Richard and she had made
their fortune.

The Stewart-Barclays left Kincardine in 1913 and moved
to Austria. Richard's good friend from Petrolia, William
McGarvey had invited him to join in a business adventure, a
new oil field discovered in Galicia. They packed up their
complete household and loaded it on the Hydrus, a cargo ship
bound for Rotterdam.

Sophia and Richard travelled with Josephine on the first
leg of their journey to England, where they parted. They
planned to meet up again in Austria. The Stewart-Barclays
never reached their destination as the train on which they were
travelling was attacked during the unrest in Europe and they
were both killed. They had no children."

"Oh, gosh! What a sad story! But tell me more about the
history of Kincardine," Rose said, as she sipped on a large glass
of wine. She still wished that she could like the man, but he
seemed so pompous and full of himself, even more so that he
was lecturing to her.

"Well, as to the overall early history of Kincardine, I can
tell you that in 1848 there were just seven families living by
the lake and they called their settlement Penatangore. The
only way to reach them was by the lake, as the forests were so
dense and hopelessly impenetrable. It wasn't until the 1850s
when the Durham/Guelph road was cut through the dense
undergrowth, that more settlers arrived.

In 1851, the name Kincardine was adopted after James
Bruce, the 8th Earl of Elgin and the 12th Earl of Kincardine
Scotland. In 1854, the Village of Kincardine was officially
incorporated. In 1874, a spur of the Wellington-Grey-Bruce
railway finally reached Kincardine, opening it up to the
outside world." John stopped talking for a minute while he

poured himself out a large glass of wine. The lecture continued after he had taken a suitable gulp of the beverage.

"In 1881, the lighthouse was built. Then, in 1901 F. E. Coombe's and James Watson opened a huge manufacturing furniture factory which remained in business right up until 1973. In 1907, the public library was opened, and in 1908 the hospital was incorporated, thanks to the generosity of Madam Gualco."

"When was Alexander Mackenzie born?" Rose asked, wondering if he was the same Alexander Mackenzie who had become Prime Minister.

John continued his lecture, his voice growing louder as he warmed to his subject.

"He was born in 1860 and no, he was not the Alexander Mackenzie we know. He was the son of a blacksmith, one of ten children. He graduated from school at the age of 17 and then he was indentured as a lawyer in Toronto with a firm called Blake, Lash, and Cassel. At 23, in 1883, he was called to the bar. When he was in his early thirties he represented a financier, William Mackenzie, probably an uncle, who had set up a company in Brazil which would provide electric tramways."

Rose had to stifle a yawn. Much as she found the whole history of Kincardine quite fascinating, John's voice droned on and on making her feel very sleepy.

"The Brazilian Traction Company was formed and Alexander, who went out to Brazil in theory just to set up the legal side of the business, stayed for the following thirty years. His partner was Francisco Gualco; they both became the most influential foreigners in Brazil. The company was consolidated in 1912 when the Sao-Paulo and Rio de Janeiro utilities were combined. The other partner in Brascan was F.

S. Pearson who sadly was drowned on the Lusitania in 1915."

John paused for dramatic effect and then resumed his lecture with added enthusiasm. "Mackenzie became President for sixteen years. The company, in 1928, had a holding of three hundred million, the largest Canadian foreign holding surpassing international nickel, Bell and aluminum. In 1915, Mackenzie financed a military hospital in the U.K. and largely funded the Red Cross. In 1919, he was knighted by King George V and to date is the only native from Bruce County ever to be knighted.

Over a period of fourteen years Sir Alexander and his wife crossed the Atlantic over one hundred times but always came back to their home, Ardloch, on Lambton Street, Kincardine. Alexander died of throat cancer in 1943.

You asked if he was the Canadian Prime Minister and I said no but in terms of putting Canada on the international map he far surpassed any man, even the Prime Minister."

Rose had been mesmerized and a little bored listening to the story of Kincardine. What a truly amazing history. Fancy one of Canada's largest corporations being based in Brazil and founded by a man from small town Kincardine. Then there was the connection to her Stewart-Barclays. Had she learnt anything that could further her enquiries into the Great Storm of 1913 and the disappearance of the ships?

"In your studies, did you come across Sinclair and Sons, an insurance broker based in Kincardine?"

John smiled slyly.

"See, I knew this was all about the lost ships. The Sinclair's were almost bankrupt after the storm and some people thought that the shock of bankruptcy might have caused the heart attack that killed the old man. Anyhow, two of the sons, Luke and John, somehow kept the business going and James, the third son, moved to Wingham and started up his own haulage business. Luke's son Jeff, as you well know, died four days ago in a boating accident. I believe that he never gave up hope in finding those lost ships. Do you know that he was diving on the day that his boat blew up?"

"No, I didn't know that," Rose said wondering how he would know that bit of information?

"Thank you for giving me such a comprehensive history lesson. You've been most helpful."

Rose went off to find Tom who was busy chatting to Dave. She overheard Dave ask Tom about Doug who had been widowed six months previously.

"He seems ok, a bit lonely if truth be known but he is slowly picking up the pieces and getting on with life."

"You play golf with him, don't you? Maybe I could join you both for a game sometime. Have you and Rose ever thought about joining the Croquet Club? Now that would also be good for Doug. I'll ask him to think about joining too."

Rose popped into the washroom and as she passed the dining room, she noticed a gorgeous Victorian silver tea service and two huge silver candelabra sitting on the sideboard. Alice and Dave must have inherited that from their mother she thought as she closed the door to the washroom.

Susan kept trying to get through to Jim's cell phone but still had no answer. She knew that one could lose cell reception out in the lake but it did concern her that after four hours he still had not answered her calls.

She drove back down to The Cottage Colony to see if there was any sign of his boat.

His car was parked in the car park and everything looked very normal. Susan's ankle had swollen up considerably and she could not put any pressure on it. The local pharmacist had very kindly bandaged it for her and she had purchased a walking stick to aid her hobbling. Every time that she limped, she cringed at the memory of the kiss with Tom. She had made a fool of herself of that she was sure, oh but that kiss had felt so good. If only Tom wasn't so happily married, but then it would be just another affair with a married man no different from Jim and her.

Fleetingly Susan thought about Jim's wife Janet and wondered if she had any inkling that her husband had been cheating on her. Jim never talked about his wife and they both pretended that she didn't exist. Still, that was all water under the bridge, and Janet could have her husband back, hopefully none the wiser for his indiscretions.

By four that afternoon Jim had not returned any of Susan's messages and she became seriously worried. Not being the type or person to do nothing she decided to call the Coast Guard:

"Look, it's probably nothing but my friend has been out on his boat for over six hours now and I'm getting a bit worried. I have no idea where he was heading and, as I said, it's probably a false alarm but if you hear anything could you please contact me on this number?" Susan rattled off her cell. "Thank you."

She put her cell phone away and hobbled back to her car. She wondered if she would be able to swim with her swollen ankle.

She had only been back in her room at The Bayfield Village Inn five minutes when her cell phone rang.

"Susan Parker here."

It was the Coast Guard's station.

"Miss Parker, we have just received a call saying that a sail-boat has been found just drifting about 2 kilometres off Grand Bend. It's a 22-foot grey and white Bayfield with the name *Tripper* on the side. We sent our rescue boat out but there was absolutely no sign of the skipper or indeed anyone on the boat. It sounds as if your friend's boat has been abandoned. We've notified the air rescue helicopter from Trenton, and they will be here shortly to start a search. The thing is, Miss Parker, the lake is very calm today, and people generally don't fall in the water when it's so calm."

Susan put her phone away and stood very still. No, Jim can't be missing, not her Jim, she thought as his large, smiling face flashed in front of her and memories of their last embrace came unbidden to her mind. No, some mistake has to have been made.

After the drinks party, Tom and Rose drove back to their house in silence. Tom still seemed preoccupied and Rose was just plain tired. Some days she really felt her age, and this was one of them. They had barely been in the house for two minutes when the phone rang. It was Jessica.

"Mom, isn't it the Bayfield Fall Fair this weekend?"

Rose had to think for a minute. She had been so busy the Fall Fair had slipped her memory. "Well, yes it is. Are you and the girls coming down to Bayfield? You're welcome to stay the night if you want or you could just drop the girls off and have a nice evening just the two of you?"

"Actually, I was hoping that you could have the girls for the weekend. We've been invited to a party Saturday night and it would save me getting a babysitter."

"Well, that's settled then. The parade starts at eleven so you had better be here by ten. See you then, love."

Rose put the phone down and turned to Tom who was

busy brushing Ben. He had taken the leash out and was getting ready to take him for a walk.

"The girls are coming this weekend. Tom, did you hear me? Please snap out of whatever is bugging you."

Tom just averted his eyes and mumbled that he would be back soon.

Rose watched as his dejected figure walked down the driveway. What on earth was wrong with him?

When Tom left the house he had no idea where he was going. He just had a burning desire to be on his own. He just felt so guilty. That kiss with Susan was so unexpected and so shameful on his part.

Ben, as usual, took the lead and he soon found himself walking down Mara Street following the dog to the harbour and onto the beach.

It was a beautiful evening. The sun was getting low over the lake casting dappled light through the trees.

The heavy leaves covering the trees down Mara Street created a tunnel which when Ella and Abby visited they always found exciting. Ben, without fail, could find tantalizing smells in the tunnel. Tom had to pull at his leash several times to bring the dog back on to the path.

At the bottom of the hill they emerged again into sunlight. There appeared to be some activity going on by the Coast Guard's building. Tom walked over and saw Susan standing next to another woman with the Coast Guard who was pointing down at a boat which looked as if it had been towed in. He recognized the boat as the one that he had seen leaving the slip earlier that day.

Tom walked over to Susan.

"What's going on here?"

Susan looked over and her eyes widened when she saw Tom.

"Oh, Tom, this apparently is Jim Reynold's boat. The Coast Guards found it drifting in the lake. This is Mr. Reynolds' wife. She drove over from Wingham. We can't find him and he hasn't been in touch with anyone."

Tom could see that Susan was trying hard to hold everything together. He guessed that Jim Reynolds was more than a 'friend' to her and seeing his wife standing next to her must feel horribly awkward for Susan. Tom reached out his hand to Jim's wife.

"Hi, I'm Susan's friend, Tom. I saw your husband go out on his boat at around 9:30 this morning. I'm so sorry. Maybe there's a simple explanation for all of this?"

Jim's wife had a hard face; her eyes didn't flinch from his when she said, "He told me that he had a meeting in London today and that he wouldn't be home until later this evening. Why would he say that and then come here and take his boat out?"

Susan looked embarrassed and shuffled her feet.

"Well, I'm the Inspector in charge of an ongoing murder investigation here in Bayfield. I'm sure that this has no connection to the case, but I will take down your details and notify you when we find your husband or have any leads as to his whereabouts. Here is my business card; I can be reached anytime on my cell phone." Susan was all brisk business.

Tom nodded to the woman and the Coast Guard and continued walking Ben down to the pier. There were a couple of fishermen sitting on stools, their rods hopefully balanced with lines in the water.

The lake used to be teeming with fish - perch, trout, and

salmon. Now it was slim pickings, one would be lucky to catch a trout but more likely nothing.

Tom stood at the end of the pier and looked out at the calm, sparkling water. He loved this quiet time of day just before the sun set.

Gulls hovered overhead; a couple of sailing boats chugged out into the lake hopeful to catch an evening breeze which Tom thought was extremely doubtful. Ben pulled at his leash, it was time to go back home and to shake off his guilt.

FOURTEEN

Susan awoke with a start. She had been dreaming of Jim and their last night together, particularly their romantic evening sail under the star lit sky. Jim was a competent sailor and had owned a boat for many years. It didn't make any sense unless Jim wanted to take his own life. But he hadn't been the least bit depressed although, of course, living a double life couldn't have been easy for him. She had always thought that he actually had enjoyed all the cloak and dagger subterfuge. Maybe there was a simple explanation, but she couldn't for the life of her fathom what it could be.

When she got to the Lion's Hall, Susan was surprised to see Rose Blair's bicycle propped up against the fence. When she entered the room, she saw her friend talking to Sergeant Flowers.

"Rose! How nice to see you! Can I be of any assistance or has Sergeant Flowers helped you?"

Rose nodded her thanks to the Sergeant and turned to Susan.

"Well, actually it doesn't matter who I talk to, but I just

thought that you should hear what I heard at a drink's party yesterday. I was told by John Bradbury, my friend Alice's son, that Jeff Sinclair had been diving for years hoping to find the lost ships from the Great Storm. It had, apparently, become something of an obsession with him. But what I found interesting was that John told me that Jeff had been diving the day of the explosion. How would he know that? I just thought that you should know. That's all."

"Thank you, Rose, we'll certainly look into it and maybe go and interview John ourselves."

Rose turned to leave and then suddenly stopped and returned to where Susan was still standing.

"If you're going to talk to him, you should catch him before he returns to Cambridge later this afternoon. Oh, and by the way, he could fill you in on the history of Kincardine, that's his area of expertise. I had the whole lecture yesterday."

Rose said her goodbyes and left the Lion's Hall just as Susan was getting her team together for the morning briefing.

"Good morning everyone! Yesterday," and here Susan paused a bit before continuing, "a Jim Reynolds from Wingham took his boat out for a sail. He left Harbour Lights at about 9:30 a.m. His boat was found drifting off the coast near Grand Bend. He was not on the boat and there was no sign of foul play.

He has not been found. Now what strikes the Coast Guard as odd is that the lake was very calm yesterday. There was no wind, so, firstly, why would anyone decide to go for a sail when there was no breeze and secondly, why would anyone just fall off a boat for no apparent reason?

Jim Reynolds was a strong swimmer and a competent sailor. His boat had all the safety equipment including a radio set that he could have used to call the Coast Guard if he was in distress.

Now the big question, is this at all connected in any way to the murder investigation or is it just one of those coincidences? I don't believe in coincidences, so we need to look deeper into this case. The other point I need to make clear is that Jim Reynolds is a friend. His wife was in Bayfield yesterday and she is naturally very worried. Be thorough but sensitive with your enquiries. We're looking for connections to our case, you all understand?"

Susan shuffled some papers around before continuing.

"Sergeant Flowers and Constable Mathieson, can you go to Wingham, talk to his wife and business acquaintances, and get a profile going on Jim Reynolds? Constable Dailey, ask around locally, show his photograph, and see if you can connect him with Ian Richards, Sam Pierce, or Jeff Sinclair. See you all tomorrow and bring me some news, everyone."

After Rose left the Lion's Building, she decided to pop into the archives to see how the map was coming on. Lena, who had a degree in graphic art, had volunteered to take the existing map that Rose had been working on and turn it into an attractive commercial proposition, one that the public might like to purchase. The Historical Society was always looking for ways to raise funds for the upkeep of the archives building. Since the new library had opened, the archives building stood alone and needed every cent that they could get in order to maintain the property.

Sure enough, Lena was busy working at her computer and so absorbed in her work that she didn't hear Rose come in.

"Hi, Lena, how are you doing?"

"Oh, just fine, do you want to look at what I've done?"

Rose nodded and Lena printed off a copy of the map. She had certainly been creative and had turned a boring map into something quite exciting. It now looked a bit like a Pirates treasure trail.

All it needed was a skull and crossbones and it could be Black Beard's famous lost treasure map.

"Look, I've included the coordinates as well as the compass points. I've used a copper plate font to give it an air of authenticity. Should I make it all sepia toned, do you think?"

Rose thought for a minute.

"Why don't we just print the final copy on beige parchment paper? I remember at school getting my students to soak their paper in tea or coffee to make it look old, that and burning the edges."

"Well, the computer can give us the same effect. Look, I've included some actual pictures of the lost ships.

I found some photographs in the files. The Carruthers is the biggest of the lot."

Rose scanned the photographs paying particular attention to the Hydrus which looked nothing special, a black hull and a central three-story cabin area presumably for the Captain and his crew, all of whom perished when the ship went down in the storm.

"I think that you've done a great job, Lena, well done. Anyway, I must be on my way as our grandchildren are coming tomorrow to stay with us and I need to do some grocery shopping."

Rose left the archives and cycled home.

Tom had gone to play golf with Doug saying that he would be back around lunch time.

She had just cycled up the driveway when a car pulled in

beside her and John Bradbury jumped out. He was wearing khaki shorts, a blue t-shirt and sported a matching blue baseball hat. Once again Rose was struck with how handsome he looked, yet there still was something about him that she didn't like.

"Just the person I wanted to see. Do you have a minute, Rose?"

Rose opened the front door and John followed. She had to put Ben into the back garden because he just wouldn't stop barking.

"Don't mind Ben, he always barks when strangers come into the house. He'll settle down in a minute. So, how can I help you?"

"Actually, I just wanted to drop off this paper I wrote on the history of Kincardine. I thought that you might appreciate a written copy as I did rather bombard you with facts and dates yesterday."

He handed Rose a folder, and she opened it to find about ten typed pages neatly stapled together.

"Thank you, John, that was very thoughtful of you. May I offer you a cup of tea or coffee?"

John nodded. "I'd love one."

"Do please take a seat. Just excuse all my papers. I like to work here in the sunroom but I'm a really messy worker."

"Don't you worry. I'm used to papers everywhere. I'll just sit here and enjoy the sunshine while you make the coffee."

Rose went off to the kitchen but as she turned her head, she could see John bending over her papers obviously interested in what was there. She tried to remember what was on the table. Definitely there was the original map of the lost ships and other research material pertaining to the Great Storm of 1913.

Why would a history buff like John be at all interested in her material? He already knew everything there was to know about the Great Storm.

Five minutes later Rose carried in a tray containing a carafe of coffee, cream, sugar, and a plate of homemade chocolate muffins.

"There you are, John. Help yourself to a muffin."

"Have you been volunteering for long at the archives?"

"Yes, since we moved here, I've been helping there about two days a week. There is so much to do. Everything has to be digitized and people keep dropping off boxes of family photographs. You know it could be a full-time job sorting everything and cataloguing it all. We've had a great student helping us this summer, but she goes back to university in a couple of weeks, so it will be just us few volunteers again."

John quickly ate one of the muffins. Wiping his mouth with one of the serviettes he said: "All communities rely heavily on the kindness and willingness of volunteers. I'm sure that you're appreciated. Well, that muffin was delicious, and the coffee was just what I needed. Right now I must get back to the family. We're heading back home to Cambridge this afternoon."

"It was nice seeing you again. Thank you for this folder of information about Kincardine," Rose said as she saw John to the door. He left, leaving Rose to ponder what was the real reason for his visit. She couldn't help disliking the man. There was just something about him and Ben obviously felt the same. She had never seen him bark so long at a stranger before.

Susan was at a loose end. Waiting to hear from the Coast Guard was painful. They had bluntly told her that if Jim had drowned, he could be washed up anywhere along the coastline or he might never be found. In a way it was a case of no news was good news. She decided to drive to Kincardine and ask a few questions and show the photographs of the three men, Ian, Sam, and Jeff. She would show the photograph of Jim too.

Janet, Jim's wife, had scanned a photograph of him and emailed it to the incident room. Susan had spent an hour reading the condensed history of the Stewart-Barclays and their relationship with the Gualcos.

There were a couple of questions that she wanted to find answers for, namely, who stood to inherit the Stewart-Barclay's money because they had died childless.

The other question was to do with the insurance brokers, Sinclair and Sons. Susan wanted to know what had happened to the sons.

She knew that after the father had died the two sons, Luke and John, had continued in the business. She also knew that Jeff was the son of Luke but what of John and James? Did they have any children?

Susan arrived in Kincardine fifty minutes later and turning left onto Durham Street she realized that she would be passing the old mansion that used to be Madam Josephine's house, called Malcolm Place. Sure enough, on her right she passed a magnificent Italianate mansion complete with a large tower or 'widow's walk'. On an impulse, Susan turned her car around and drove up the driveway to Malcolm Place.

There was a sign that said, *Nursing Home*. It was always such a shame to see so many big, old homes being converted into retirement or nursing homes mainly because of the upkeep and expense of owning a substantial mansion. Susan knocked on the door and was shown into a huge and beautiful hallway. The floor was spectacular, cherry wood inlaid with golden teak strips, panels of walnut wood and a magnificent Italian chandelier suspended from the ceiling by a heavy chain. Ornate wrought-iron railings formed a balcony which looked out over the hallway. Marble statues nestled in little alcoves recessed into the wall.

The proprietor, Mrs. Strobe, was a lovely lady who, when Susan explained about the enquiry, was more than willing to help.

"You say the Stewart-Barclays moved here because his wife, Sophia, had a sister living in Kincardine? Well, she would be long past by now but if she had children and if they had remained living in Kincardine, they would be up in their nineties by now. I just wonder if Mrs. Williams in Room 8 might know anything about Sophia's sister. She's a bit deaf but otherwise completely alert. Here, follow me and I'll show you to her room."

Mrs. Williams sat by the window of a very light and spacious bedroom. She looked almost doll-like, very diminutive with a shock of thick, white hair.

"Mrs. Williams, I have a visitor for you. This is Ms. Parker. She's with the police from the Special Crimes Unit in London."

Mrs. Williams turned to look at Susan and in a loud and imperious voice said:

"Special crimes, what's so special about crimes? Speak up, girl."

Susan couldn't stop herself from smiling.

"I'm currently investigating a murder. We think that there is some connection to the lost ships from the Great Storm of 1913. I'm trying to track down any relatives of the Stewart-

Barclays. I also want to know what happened to the insurance broker Sinclair and Sons?"

Susan wondered if the old lady had heard her, as she seemed to go very still and quiet.

She then fairly shouted out, "There was a sister. I reckon my mother knew her, Polish she was. Anyway, if I recall, she came into a huge sum of money. My mother said that it went to her head and that no good came of her. The thing is, the war came, and this sister lost not only her husband but her two sons. It was a terrible war. Let me think, there was a daughter who survived and, I believe, inherited the lot when her mother passed away. Actually, I remember telling all of this to a nice young man just a few weeks ago. He said that he was a journalist doing research into the influential families of Bruce County."

"Well, that's interesting. Did he give his name?"

"Oh, I'm not sure. It could have been James, maybe Jim or possibly John. It began with 'J', anyway."

Susan pulled out the photographs she had of Sam, Ian, Jeff, and Jim and handed them over to Mrs. Williams.

"Were any of these men the man who spoke to you?"

Mrs. Williams studied each photograph carefully. Finally, she handed them back to Susan.

"No, he was about those lads' age," she said, pointing to Ian and Sam, "But much better looking, but these," she said, picking up the pictures of Jeff and Jim, "look familiar too."

Susan thanked her and put the photographs away.

"Now, do you know anything about the Sinclair boys? I understand that Sinclair and Sons almost went bankrupt in 1913 and that the father died the following year leaving his sons to run the business. Have you any recollection of Sinclair and Sons?"

Mrs. Williams went quiet while she thought, and once again the silence seemed to last forever.

"Well, of course I wasn't born until 1917, by which time Mr. Sinclair had already passed on, but I can tell you that the Sinclair family had nothing but tragedy thrust upon them.

Of the three sons Luke, James, and John, only Luke and John continued to run the family business. Both lads enlisted to fight in the First World War. John was killed leaving a young widow and a little daughter. Luke came home traumatised and was never the same again.

His wife, Eleanor, died of polio in 1927. I was ten then and there was a terrible outbreak of polio that year. Luke remarried in 1935 and they had a son, Jeff, in 1940. Luke died in 1950 of a massive heart attack. He was sixty.

The youngest son, James, went into haulage and left Kincardine. I believe I heard that he moved to Wingham. More tragedy there! I believe two of his sons drowned in the lake and his wife died ostensibly of a broken heart.

James remarried in 1951 and had another son, Jimmy. James died in a truck accident in 1953. So you see, the Sinclair family seems to have been cursed."

Wow, thought Susan, *what an amazing mind*. The old dear was so sharp and based on her date of birth she had to be 96. What a trooper. She got up to leave.

"Thank you so much, you have been most helpful."

"Oh, but this has been so exciting! I've never been part of a murder enquiry."

Susan left the beautiful house which, if walls could talk, would be able to tell an amazing story. Apparently, Madam Josephine Gualco had moved from Kincardine back to Montreal after years of donating to the town that she loved.

Over the years, she had paid for the hospital, a golf course, playgrounds, and schools. She had been a true philanthropist but due to bad investments, had been forced to leave Kincardine penniless and to sell off her beautiful house to pay back taxes owed.

Josephine Gualco had emigrated from Poland and it was that, apart from the immediate circles she moved in, that had drawn Sophia Stewart-Barclay and her together into a deep friendship. Interestingly, Helena McGarvey was also Polish and, of course, Sophia and Helena had become good friends too.

Susan drove back to Bayfield pondering on all that she had learnt from Mrs. Williams.

Tom arrived home shortly after John Bradbury had left. The tray with the coffee, cream and muffins was still on the table. Rose was making a cheese frittata for their lunch.

"Oh, hi darling, did you have a good game of golf?"

"Yes, Dave joined Doug and me. In fact, we've been invited to a croquet club cocktail party tonight at Dave's. I said that we would come at about 5:30."

"Gosh, we were just at Alice and Dave's. Oh well, we've got nothing planned for this evening. Just as well it's tonight and not tomorrow, as Ella and Abby will be here. Oh, by the way Tom, John, Alice and Dave's son, popped over and Ben went crazy. I don't know what got into him, I had to put him in the garden as he was barking so much."

"What did he come around for?"

"Supposedly to give me some history notes, but I think that he was snooping around my papers. I have to say that I don't like him one single bit."

"Oh, well, love, it takes all sorts. Alice and Dave seem nice enough."

"Yes, Alice is a sweetheart."

"So, you're alright about tonight?"

"Oh, yes, I love parties and we'll get to meet the Croquet Club set. Is Doug going to come?"

"Yes, I said that we would pick him up. That way he can't wriggle out of coming, and it will do him good to get out."

Rose took the frittata out of the oven, tossed the salad, and called Tom to the table for lunch. Over their lunch, they discussed the Croquet Club. They had both once cycled down David Street to the Croquet Club, which was hidden at the end of the road behind the cemetery. Rose had always considered Croquet a really old-fashioned game, but the people who played really seemed to enjoy it.

To Rose, the game looked like a mixture between golf and lawn bowls. Several of her bridge buddies were Croquet Club members; maybe it was time that Tom and she joined.

Tuyl Street was full of cars parked at the side of the road. Alice and Dave's house, well, their garden, was teaming with people mostly dressed in their whites, so much so, that Rose felt conspicuous wearing her yellow summer dress; in fact, she suddenly realised that it was the same dress she had worn the last time they had visited Alice and Dave.

One thing that Rose intended to do was to pop into the house and have another look at the silver tea service and the candelabra. She thought that she could probably take some photos of the silver pieces using Tom's iPhone; it certainly would be easier than trying to recall what they looked like in detail afterwards.

An hour into the cocktail party, Rose made the excuse of needing to use the washroom. Both Alice and Dave were busy hosting, and the drinks and food had been set up under a canopy overlooking the lake some distance from the house. She should be undisturbed in her mission to photograph the silver.

Walking into the dining room, she was once again struck by the magnificence of the silver, in particular the ornate candelabras. Rose knew a bit about silver. It was one of her hobbies searching out the silversmith's hallmark on the underside of articles of silver. Nowadays, having the internet made it so much easier. The hallmark was like an equivalent bar-code which could tell the whole history, who, where, and when, it was made, and Rose fully intended to find more about Alice and Dave's silverware even though what she was doing wasn't strictly ethical.

Rose managed to take her photographs and was just closing the door to the dining room when Alice appeared.

"Are you looking for the washroom, Rose? It's through there."

Rose felt a pang of guilt but decided to brazen it out.

"Alice, I couldn't help but notice your lovely silver tea set and candelabras in the dining room. They look quite old. Did you inherit them from your mother?"

"Oh, no, Rose. John gave Dave and me this silver tea set on our wedding anniversary. He said that he bought it from a flea market outside of London. The candelabras were also a present from John. He likes searching out antiques."

"Well, you are lucky, they're lovely."

"I must go back to the party. When you're finished, come out and meet the Croquet Club president. He'll probably ask you to join but don't worry if you don't want to, there's no pressure and nobody would be offended."

Rose smiled and thanked Alice. She was such a sweet friend and maybe Tom and she might join the Croquet Club after all, as everyone seemed very welcoming.

They got home at eight that evening. There was a message flashing on the telephone from Anne.

"Mom, Dad, I'm catching the train to Stratford. I will be arriving around eleven tomorrow morning. Hope it's ok if I stay for the weekend. Love you, see you tomorrow.

Tom listened to the message while Rose let Ben out into the garden.

"What time is Jessica bringing the girls over?"

"Oh, I told her to get here before ten as the parade starts at eleven."

"Well, I'll go and pick up Ann from Stratford. I don't mind if I miss the parade this year. She's staying for the weekend."

It never rains, but it pours, Rose thought as she opened the fridge and thought about what she would cook for the following day. Anne was a vegetarian, and that always gave Rose pause for thought. Normally she would make a lentil curry or something spicy, but Ella and Abby wouldn't eat curry. She decided that a potato and cheese bake served with a crusty baguette and a nice tossed salad would do the trick. There were still some chocolate muffins left over, and there was always ice cream in the freezer.

With the meal planned, Rose sat down to her computer and got out Tom's iPhone.

"Tom, how do I download these photos?"

What would she do without Tom, Rose thought for the hundredth time. She was pretty useless with anything technical.

Twenty minutes later, Rose was looking at the ten or more photographs she had taken, in particular the underside of the teapot and candelabras showing the embossed silver hallmarks.

She printed off the pictures and then went onto the internet to find the silver Hallmark information. By comparing the hallmarks listed on the screen with those in the pictures she had taken, Rose was able to establish that the silversmith was from Birmingham, England and the date manufactured was 1898.

Furthermore, the mark told her that the silver in question was 'one of a kind', not part of a commercial manufacturing job. In fact, the silver tea set and candelabras looked as if they were a rare find.

Rose wondered if there was any way to establish who the original owners had been. She would have to think about that and conduct a bit of research.

FIFTEEN

Susan felt quite like a new woman now that the swelling on her ankle had gone down. She managed to swim fifty lengths of the pool and now felt ready to face the day. She could feel it in her bones that they were closing in on the murderer. She drove to the Lion's Hall, ready to brief her team.

"Good morning everyone. First, let us have your report, Sergeant Flowers."

"Right, well, Constable Mathieson and I went to Wingham and showed our photographs around. We had quite a few people recognise Jim Reynolds, and that is understandable, as he lives in Wingham. In Coffee Cultures the girl behind the counter thought that she had seen Jeff Sinclair and Jim Reynolds sitting at a table drinking coffee. The guy at the Shell Garage also thought that he recognized Jim and Jeff filling up gas in a car. Now Janet Reynolds said that she had overheard Jim talking to someone called Jeff. It does seem to appear that the two men knew each other. Janet also reckons that Jim was cheating on her. She has no proof, but he seemed to be away a lot on so called conferences, which didn't always check out.

The other interesting piece of information is that Jim Reynolds' business is about to go into receivership. Janet knows nothing about this. She is a nurse at the local hospital and it does appear that they have been living primarily off her income for quite a while now. That concludes my report."

"Thank you, Sergeant. Now, Constable Dailey, anything more on the local scene?"

"Well, I showed photographs of all four men, and the results were interesting. Down at Harbour Lights, lots of people recognized Jim. Several people thought that they had seen the two men, Jeff and Jim, sailing together. Nobody saw Ian or Sam with Jim Reynolds. It does appear that Jim and Jeff knew each other. Jim had been staying at The Cottage Colony for the week prior to his disappearance. He was with another woman and was seen several times at The Docks and also at The Black Dog. That concludes my report."

Susan thought quickly. The problem was if she was to disclose that she was having an affair with Jim, the case would probably be compromised.

If she didn't come clean with the truth, it would be seen that she was holding back information from a crime scene and that was actually breaking the law. She was saved from making her decision when her cell phone rang. The body of Sam Pierce had been found.

Richard Watson took his dog, Bambi, for a walk every morning and evening, and every day he took the same route up Jowett's Grove Road past the Harbour Court Condominiums and then down a private road to the beach. Enroute, he always passed an old, disused well which had been boarded up for years. For the past few days his dog had persistently pulled on his leash and dragged Richard over to the old well, which had begun to smell dreadfully like something decomposing.

On the third day, the stench was so appalling that Richard called in the municipality. They sent someone to check out the well and on opening it they had found the body of a man, which later was confirmed as being that of Sam Pierce.

Susan and her team waited for both the forensic and the pathologist's teams to arrive from London. They had taped off the area, covered the body and were huddled together in deep conversation.

"This is obviously Sam Pierce. Other than a cut on his head and general bruising on his body, there seem no obvious signs of the cause of death. We will have to wait for both forensic and pathology to send in their results. At least we now have confirmation of another murder. It appears, gentlemen, that we have three, possibly four homicides to investigate. We have much work to do. Constable Dailey, stay here and wait for the coroner and forensics team to arrive. Sergeant Flowers and Constable Mathieson, keep showing those photographs, particularly the one of Jim Reynolds. Somehow all four men are linked. Go to it and dig deeper. These crimes must be solved soon."

Susan drove back to the Lion's Hall and prepared to type up her report on the latest murder.

Tom left the house to drive to Stratford to pick up their daughter Anne from the station. Not long after his departure, Jessica arrived with Abby and Ella. The two little girls burst out of the car and in through the front door like exploding fireworks.

"Grandma, oh Grandma, Mummy said that we can spend the night with you and Grandpa. Where is Grandpa?"

Abby, dressed in a little pink sundress, had pulled off her pink spotted floppy hat and was holding a huge bag which fairly dwarfed her little body.

"Oh, darling, put that big bag down and come and give Grandma a hug. Grandpa's gone to the station to pick up Aunty Anne."

Ella, who had been standing quietly, thumb in her mouth, ran over to Rose and jumped into her arms. Abby, not to be outsmarted, grabbed Rose's legs and clung to her like a limpet.

Jessica called out to the girls: "Abby, Ella, leave Grandma alone. Now go and put your bags in the bedroom and come back to give me a kiss. I have to leave before the roads get closed off for the Bayfield Fall Parade."

Abby and Ella obeyed their mother and quickly returned to give her a kiss and wave her goodbye.

"Now, girls, let's have some cookies and milk, and then we're going to walk over to Main Street and watch the parade.

"Grandma, can Ben come too?"

Rose looked at Ben, who had been sitting rather too close to the plate of cookies.

"Why, yes, of course he can come. Now hurry up and eat your cookies."

Main Street was positively packed with people. Rose managed to secure a good spot for the girls and Ben to watch the parade. They conveniently stood in front of the ice cream parlour and naturally Rose bought them all an ice cream, including a small one for Ben.

The Police cars blared their sirens, the fire truck honked its horn, bagpipes started to play and the marching band proceeded to parade down the street. There followed float after float, the Shriners toy - like cars weaving in and out and candy being liberally tossed to the crowds. Abby and Ella caught the sweets and stored their bootie in their pockets. Even Ben managed to catch a few candies in his mouth and devoured them with one chomp of his jaws. Rose looked around to see if she could recognize any of her friends.

Across the road, in front of The Little Inn, Alice and Dave stood watching the parade. Rose couldn't see their son, John, and his family.

They probably didn't want to drive back to Bayfield again so soon after their last visit. Rose was just focusing on 'The Lion's Club's' float when she could have sworn that she saw Jim, Susan's friend, standing next to the notice board in front of the library.

Her view was partially blocked by the crowds of people, but for one fleeting moment she thought that she had seen him. Hadn't Tom told her that Jim's boat had been found drifting in the lake and that Jim himself had disappeared? Perhaps the man she had seen just looked like him. After all, she had only met him once before, and that was at The Docks over a week ago.

She put this to the back of her mind and continued to wave at the people on the floats. She wondered if Tom would be back soon and then she wondered about Anne, the daughter that concerned her the most, the 'hopeless-in-love' girl who always had such high hopes and then was permanently having her dreams crushed. *Poor love*, Rose thought again, *my poor misguided daughter*. When would she ever learn?

During the drive back to Bayfield from Stratford, Tom listened patiently to Anne as she ranted and raved about Seth. Tom had heard it all before. How could he advise his daughter, who seemed hell bent on making the same mistakes time and time again, in her choice of men?

The trouble with Anne was, she had a big heart. She loved the underdog, always thought that she would be able to change what to everyone else was past changing.

Their lovely, talented, intelligent daughter should have learnt by now that people rarely changed, and she would either have to accept Seth the way he was or move on, end of story.

They arrived home just as Rose, Abby, Ella, and Ben turned into Bayfield Terrace. Anne jumped out of the car and ran to greet her little nieces.

"Abby, Ella, give your aunty a kiss." The girls, who absolutely adored their Aunty Anne, leapt into her open arms. She swung Ella onto her shoulders and grabbed Abby by her hand.

"Oh, we're going to have such fun on the beach today!"

The girls squealed with delight. Rose and Tom followed them into the house, which, Tom observed wryly, had not been locked up.

Over lunch, Abby and Ella did not stop talking and Anne encouraged them. Ben lay under the table, willing scraps of food to come his way.

"Anyone for ice cream?" Rose asked as she loaded up the dishwasher and opened up the fridge.

"Do you have any ice lollies, Grandma?" Ella asked plaintively, as she jumped down from the table and padded over to the freezer.

"I'd like a blue one."

"Where are your manners, young lady? What do you say?"

"Please and thank you, Grandma."

Rose smiled. She was a stickler for manners, and a little 'please and thank you' went a long way in her book.

After lunch Anne said that she would take the girls down to the beach, leaving Tom and Rose to have some quiet time together. Rose made a pot of tea and they both sat down together on the sofa in the sunroom.

"Tom, how could I track down who the silver pieces were originally made for? I know the date and the silversmith. Where do I go next?"

Tom thought for a while and then he said:

"Well, Sotheby's would be your best bet. They employ specialists from all over the world. You might try them first and see what happens."

Later on, after Tom was happily ensconced in front of the television watching his beloved football, Rose sent an email with photograph attachments to Sotheby's. It was Saturday, and so she really didn't expect to hear from them before Monday.

Susan spent most of the day feeling unsure of what her next move should be. She was still uncertain whether she should reveal her involvement with Jim Reynolds. Finally, after much thought, she tapped in the Chief Inspector's cell number.

"Chief Inspector Roper speaking."

"Oh, umm, sir, can I meet up with you soon? I need to discuss an important issue pertaining to the case. Something that could potentially be a conflict of interest that I can't discuss over the phone."

"Why, yes, Susan, I'm actually free first thing Monday morning, 9:00 a.m. prompt."

"Yes, sir, I'll be there."

Susan sat quietly, thinking. What on earth was Jim up to? Deciding that she couldn't just sit around idly waiting for the case to unfold, she made up her mind to go down to the marina and take another look at Jim's boat. No sign of foul play had been found, but maybe she might find something that could point out and explain away his disappearance.

The cabin was very neat, ship shape, Susan thought as she ducked her head and looked into the sleeping quarters in the ship's bow. She opened a few drawers, closed them, and then picked up a paperback book sitting on top of the storage shelves.

Jim had been reading Will Ferguson's *Canadian Pie*. Susan flicked through it and was about to lay it down when a thin brown envelope fell to the floor.

The envelope was addressed to a Mr. Stewart-Barclay Esq. and it was written in beautiful, neat copperplate writing.

Susan opened the envelope and pulled out a piece of brittle, yellowing paper. It looked like an inventory of sorts, a list of contents presumably of the Stewart-Barclay's estate.

This must be what was stolen from Rose and Tom's home, she thought as she tucked the ledger back into the envelope. What was Jim doing with this, and more to the point, why would he have stolen it? How could you think that you know someone when really you didn't know them at all?

Susan felt sick to the stomach. To think that she had been seduced by a man who had no scruples, could actually walk into someone's house and even possibly be implicated in the murder. What on earth had she got herself into and why had she, of all people, not known that he was a sham?

Abby and Ella finally went to sleep after both Rose and Anne had read them five bedtime stories.

Tom poured each of them a large glass of wine. He had also laid out some cheese and crackers on the coffee table.

"Thank you, darling, just what the doctor ordered. Come and sit down next to me and Anne and fill us in with what's going on in your life?"

Anne sipped her wine and grimaced. She was not a wine drinker, much preferring good, strong ale.

"Well, Seth and I are over, but I don't want to talk about that. My big news is that I've decided to move to Halifax. In fact, I've just accepted a position at Dalhousie. I need a fresh start and I think that this is the perfect opportunity for me to reinvent myself."

"Gosh, that is a big step to make, a new job, new city, new life. Congratulations, love, when do you leave?" Tom said, while refilling Rose and his wine glasses.

"I have to be on campus for fresher week which starts on September 2nd. Next week I leave Toronto. I'm going to sublet my apartment to Seth, so I'll leave all my furniture. I've been online looking at apartments in Halifax, and I've found one that's fully furnished within walking distance of the university, and it's under $1,000 a month. So, that's my big news."

"Well, let's make a toast to you. May you settle down well and love your new job. Cheers."

Tom and Rose toasted their daughter, and they spent the rest of the evening talking about Nova Scotia and New Brunswick. Already, they were planning a visit and Anne hadn't even left.

SIXTEEN

The girls woke up early on Sunday morning and came running into Tom and Rose's bedroom. Rose sat up and looked at her watch and groaned. It was only six o'clock.

"Good morning, Abby, good morning Ella, do you want to jump into bed with us?" She lifted the warm bed covers and Abby and Ella snuggled up between Tom and her. Ben was snoring softly in his dog bed, and Tom hadn't even stirred. Rose thought that the girls had gone back to sleep when Abby piped up in a loud voice.

"We saw a man. He was in the garden, Grandma, and Ella was frightened. He looked like a bad man. He tried to come into the house, Grandma. We heard him. He had a flashlight, and he was shining it everywhere."

Rose felt really alarmed. She grabbed Tom's arm and shook it.

"Tom, the girls saw a man in our garden. Tom, wake up and listen." Finally he sat up and Abby regaled him with her story, which seemed to have been somewhat embellished in the retelling.

"Ella thought that he was a giant. I think that he was a monster come to eat Ella up."

Tom got out of bed and went to the window. Pulling back the blinds, he looked out into the garden. The dawn was breaking, and it was very still, with a slight mist rising from the ground. As he was about to turn, something caught his eye. He glanced back and looked more closely. Down at the bottom of the garden, hanging from one of the pear trees, was what looked like a body suspended by a rope.

"What is it, Tom, did you see something?"

Tom put his finger to his mouth, indicating that she should say nothing more. He quickly slipped on a pair of shoes. Grabbing his dressing gown, he quietly let himself out into the garden. Walking over the dewy grass, he felt a slight chill in the air. Fall was definitely on its way.

As he approached the object, it became clear that what was hanging from the tree was not a body, but what looked like an oversized rag doll. When he got closer, a crude version of a scarecrow had been tied together using a jacket and a pair of trousers and a cotton pillowcase stuffed to replicate a head.

A length of yellow nylon cord had been looped around the neck so that it appeared to look like a child hanging.

A light breeze slowly sprang up, and the body turned, revealing a handwritten note pinned to the jacket.

In large capitals, using a black marker, someone had scrawled: "THIS COULD BE YOU."

Tom's first reaction was to cut it down, but just as he was about to, he recalled the other incidents that had been happening in the village. He should maybe contact the police.

Hurrying back into the kitchen, he telephoned Susan's cell number. Susan picked up on the second ring.

"Inspector Parker speaking, how can I help you?"

Susan had been woken up with a jolt by her cell phone ringing sharply in her ear. It was Tom Blair, and he had sounded very agitated. Foregoing her morning swim, she hurriedly got dressed and was at the Blair's house within ten minutes of receiving the call.

Tom showed her into the back garden, and she gasped when she saw the object swinging from the tree at the bottom of the garden. Initially she thought that it was a child, but on closer inspection she immediately saw that it was some sort of scarecrow with a yellow nylon rope around its neck. She reached out to steady the swinging effigy and read the crude note pinned to the jacket.

"Tom, this is grotesque and sinister. It is obviously a serious warning to you and Rose. Look, I'll get the team over to see if they can lift any footprints from around the house. They'll come and photograph this and we'll get that yellow rope analysed too. I'm so sorry that this should happen to you."

Tom had told Rose about the hanging scarecrow and had suggested she distract the girls for a few hours. It was only seven o'clock in the morning, Anne was still sound asleep. Rose kept all the blinds in the house closed and suggested to Abby and Ella that they might like to watch television while she made breakfast for them.

Ben started barking when the police arrived and Abby, sharp as ever, said, "Grandma, why is Ben barking? Is it that monster-man in the garden?"

"No, darling, don't worry about Ben. He just wants Grandpa to take him for a walk and he will in a minute."

Rose made French toast or 'eggy bread' as Ella liked to call it, and she put yoghurt and blueberries in little glass bowls for all of them. There was still no sign of Anne getting up, so Rose decided to let her sleep in. She called Tom in for breakfast. He had been outside talking to Susan. Rose was dying to hear what was going on but didn't want to draw attention to anything that would alarm the girls.

The police left just as Anne was getting up.

"Mom, what were the police doing here?"

Rose put her finger to her lips and beckoned Anne into the sun lounge out of earshot of the little girls. She told Anne about the hanging scarecrow and the threatening note.

"That's just plain creepy. What pervert would do that in Bayfield of all places?"

Rose didn't want to tell her daughter about the other break-in, although her sister Jessica had already told Anne about the murder.

"You and Dad must be careful. If there's some whacko out there, who knows what he'll do next?"

"Darling, we'll be just fine. I'm sure that the police will get to the bottom of this. It's probably some kids playing a prank on us."

Rose sounded more confident than she actually felt. The nasty note had shaken her more than the swinging effigy. How could this be happening to them in sleepy old Bayfield?

Susan arrived at the Lion's Hall a little later than usual. She had stopped at Da Vinci's for coffee but had stayed on for breakfast. They made the most delicious pancakes.

The team was waiting.

"Good morning, everyone. Well, we all had an early start today, so let's get this meeting over with quickly so that we can get on with the investigation.

Yesterday, I went over to the Harbour Lights Marina and had another look at Jim Reynolds' boat. I found, tucked in a paperback book, a brown envelope containing the ship's manifest for the Hydrus. If you remember, this had been stolen from Tom and Rose Blair's house ten days ago.

We now have another link. It is obvious that Jim Reynolds was connected to the other men, who also appeared to be interested in the manifest.

This morning the same couple, Rose and Tom, received a distinct warning, a grim one at that. The big question is who left the warning? Now, Sergeant Flowers, anything more to report?"

"Yes, ma'am! We went back to Wingham to speak to Janet Reynolds. She told us that Jim was a keen scuba diver and had dived in Lake Huron on more than one occasion. She also said that he had been reading up on The Great Storm of 1913. We interviewed some of his employees and they all spoke well of him.

They knew that the business was struggling, but then a lot of printers are feeling the pinch. That is all we have to report."

"Constable Dailey, have you anything to report?"

"Yes, ma'am. I'm not sure if it's relevant but when I was asking around at the marina yesterday, one of the boaters mentioned that his red inflatable dinghy had gone missing. I asked around at the Coast Guard and they called Grand Bend and apparently a red dinghy was found washed up on the shore at St. Joseph's. The proprietors of Brentwood-on-the-Beach telephoned the Grand Bend Coast Guard."

"Thank you, Constable. Now gentlemen, we need to concentrate on finding the person or persons who left the scarecrow effigy and the sinister note at Rose and Tom Blair's house. Constable Dailey, put together a list of who has bought yellow nylon rope from any hardware store here in Bayfield, Clinton, Grand Bend or Goderich. Flowers and Mathieson, go back to Wingham and dig deeper into the Reynolds family history. I want to know all there is to know about them. For myself, I still feel that these murders are all connected somehow to Kincardine. Tomorrow morning, I need to go to London first thing in the morning so we will have our briefing in the afternoon at 2:00 p.m. Go to it everyone."

Tom, Rose, Anne, and the girls went for a lovely sail after lunch. There was just enough breeze to billow out the sails. The water sparkled like a kaleidoscope of diamonds, and the sky was a clear, bright blue. In other words, a perfect summer's day!

Rose packed a thermos of coffee, some homemade oatmeal cookies, some lemonade, and some cubes of cheese and crackers. Abby and Ella wore their snug fitting life vests and Anne sat between them in the cockpit of the boat singing nursery rhymes, making up the words as she went along.

The fresh air was doing her so much good, she thought. Living in Toronto, Anne rarely went down to the lake even though the Harbour Front was really quite lovely.

Jessica was picking the girls up at four and Anne had to catch the eight o'clock train from Stratford. Rose wasn't sure if Jessica would be staying for dinner or not, but she made a large lasagna which would feed at least six and, of course, she had made a vegetarian lasagna for Anne. Sailing had been Tom's idea and Rose was pleased that he had suggested that they get out of the house. The stiff wind had helped blow away any thoughts of the sinister note left behind pinned onto the grotesque doll. Whoever left it must be a pretty sick person, Rose thought and refused to dwell on the subject anymore.

They got back to the house at 3:30p.m. Both Abby and Ella were tired. Anne lay on the bed with them and started to read them a story while Rose put the kettle on for tea. Tom took Ben out for a quick walk.

When Jessica arrived half an hour later the house was very quiet. Tom and Rose were sitting in the sun lounge having their tea, Anne was still in the bedroom reading stories to the girls and Ben was snoring away in his dog basket.

"Wow, how peaceful it is here."

Jessica smiled as she plonked herself down on the sofa next to Rose.

"Did you and Rob have a good time without the kids, darling?"

"Yes, the party was great but I'm a bit hungover at the moment."

"Are you going to stay for dinner?"

"Well, actually, mom, I thought that I'd just pick up the girls and run. Rob and I started painting the kitchen and I must go back to help finish it, so thanks all the same."

Rose nodded and called Abby and Ella.

"Mummy, we went sailing on Grandpa's boat," Abby shouted. Ella said, "There was a man in the garden. He was a monster!"

Jessica looked at Rose questioningly.

"Oh, dear, I'll tell you all about it later, love. Right now, do you want a nice cup of tea or would you like me to make a pot of coffee?"

"Did someone say coffee?" Anne said as she emerged from the bedroom. "I'd love a cup. Oh, hi, Jess, when did you get here?"

"I've just arrived, so what's up?"

The two sisters started chatting away, and Rose made some coffee and poured out milk for the girls. On days like this, when she was surrounded by the ones she loved, Rose felt like the luckiest woman alive. To love and to be loved! What more could anyone ask for?

SEVENTEEN

Susan drove to London with a sinking feeling in her stomach. She just prayed that she wouldn't be taken off the case because of her relationship with Jim. On the plus side, she knew that she was doing the right thing coming clean to the Chief. Whatever the outcome, she would accept the consequences with dignity.

She pulled up in front of the Serious Crimes Unit Headquarters. She had five minutes to go to the washroom and freshen up before her meeting with the Inspector. Susan looked at herself in the mirror. Did she look like a 'Scarlet' woman? She had deliberately worn a rather severe grey jacket over a pale blue shirt with matching grey pants. She put some lipstick on and brushed her hair, took a deep breath, and marched confidently into the Chief's office.

Susan had decided to just say it as it was and not try to cover up her relationship with Jim.

The chief listened quietly as she blustered on, and then, when she had finished, he sat there for what felt like an eternity before he finally spoke.

"What you have told me could have happened to anyone and the way I see it, you, or indeed nobody in the village, had any idea that this Jim Reynolds was up to no good. Whether your case has been compromised by your personal involvement with whom now appears to be your prime suspect, well, I think that we can overlook your relationship on the condition, of course, that it is indeed over. We will say no more on the subject. However, we do need to review the investigation and where it stands at the moment."

The Chief coughed and shifted in his chair looking sharply at Susan as she fairly squirmed in her seat. "You have the two dead men and the third boat explosion victim all presumably connected to this Jim Reynolds? Then there is the drifting boat and a red inflatable dinghy found on the shores of St. Joseph's.

It appears that your prime suspect might have staged his supposed drowning and could now be roaming free heaven knows where. He could be on his way to Timbuktu by now. Have you alerted the border guards and the airports?"

Susan nodded her head, and he continued,

"It strikes me, Susan, that your case is closed in as much as you now know who the perpetrator of the crime is. You just have to find him. I suggest that you wind up the case, disband your team, and head back to London. If need be, we can always get Interpol involved in the search for Jim Reynolds."

"Well, sir, we do have a few loose ends to tie up. Although the motivation for the murders is linked to the lost ships of the Great Storm of 1913 and in particularly one ship the Hydrus, we still do not know why the men were murdered."

The Chief Superintendent thought for a while.

"You may never know the full motive if we don't succeed in catching up with this Jim Reynolds character. Tie up those loose ends, Inspector, and write it all up in a final report and be back in London by Friday. Good day, Inspector."

Susan drove back to Bayfield in one sense feeling relieved that she had not been severely reprimanded for her relationship with Jim, but, on the other hand she felt a degree of frustration. The case did not feel conclusive. There were still far too many loose ends and unanswered questions and she now had only four days to wrap it all up and return to London.

Rose was thrilled when she opened her emails that morning and found one from Sotheby's. They had sent her a catalogue of Victorian Silverware sold at auctions over the past decade. She clicked through the pages until she came to the candelabras section. There were over one hundred in all different shapes and sizes.

On page 60 she found an identical pair to those she had photographed from Alice and Dave's house.

The candelabra in the catalogue were listed as part of the Stewart-Barclays estate, sold in 2003. Rose gulped when she saw the date.

Just how could the Stewart-Barclays candelabra have found their way into a Sotheby's collection when the whole container load of household contents belonging to the Stewart-Barclays had disappeared along with the ship in the Great Storm of 1913?

She continued looking through the catalogue and found the silver tea service and a number of other silver chafing dishes and bowls all bearing the Stewart-Barclays family crest and all sold in 2003.

Well, that puts all my theories of diving for treasure out of the window, Rose thought as she printed off a copy of the catalogue to show Tom and Susan. Another thought occurred to her as she logged out of the computer.

John Bradbury had told his parents that he had purchased the silverware from a flea market outside of London. Why would he deliberately lie to his parents?

The other thing that crossed Rose's mind was the price that the silverware was listed at. The reserves on the candelabra were set at $5,000 each and the tea service at $25,000. Just where would John get that sort of money to buy these items? *Certainly not on a teacher's salary*, Rose thought as she folded the printed pages and tucked them into her bag.

She would cycle over to the archives and then drop into the Lion's Hall and speak to Susan.

"Right, good afternoon everyone. Let's get straight down to business. The Chief wants this case wrapped up by the end of the week. We all must report for duty back In London next Monday, so let's get on with it. Sergeant Flowers and Constable Mathieson, what have you got for us?"

Sergeant Flowers stood up and got ready to speak.

"We really dug deep, ma'am, and came up with some interesting facts. Firstly, our man Jim is a Sinclair. His mother remarried when he was only about three. She had been married to James Sinclair after his first wife supposedly died of a broken heart when their two sons drowned in Lake Huron. They were married for ten years and little Jimmy was born. James Sinclair died of a massive heart attack and his widow, Jim's mom, married Angus Reynolds. Jim took his stepdad's name. So, you see, Jeff and Jim were cousins."

Sergeant Flowers drew out his notebook and prepared to read from it. "The other piece of information we found interesting was the presence of two numbered bank accounts linked to Jim's business through a complex arrangement of numbered holding companies.

We found that Jim's business account was in bankruptcy. According to the bank he owed people left, right and centre, but the hidden bank accounts showed huge sums of money.

In one account with CIBC, there is over one million dollars, and the other account with TD shows $800,000. There have, however, been regular withdrawals each month for the past ten years."

Sergeant Flowers voice suddenly sounded quite animated as he warmed to his subject. "Now this is where it really gets interesting. $2,000 a month has been paid into a Cambridge Bank account in the name of John Bradbury."

Susan clapped her hands. "Great work. Well, we'll be having a little talk with Mr. Bradbury. I believe his parents live in Bayfield. Constable Dailey, anything to report?"

"Yes, ma'am, it's about the red dingy. A man matching Jim Reynolds description, was seen walking down the beach at St. Joseph's in the early hours of the morning by Mrs. Jackson who was out taking her morning swim in the lake. She saw the man get out of the red dingy, pull it onto the beach and then walk away. She thought that he might be a guest staying at Brentwood-on-the-Beach Guest House. Anyway, that's all I have to report."

"Thank you, Constable. Right, well we are at last making progress. Sergeant Flowers, you and I will take a drive to Cambridge to interview John Bradbury, and Constable Mathieson, drive up to Kincardine and delve more deeply into Sinclair and Sons and find out who stood to inherit the Stewart-Barclay's fortune when they died? Constable Dailey, keep showing the photographs around locally. What about the yellow nylon rope, any results from that?"

"I spoke to all the hardware stores in this area. There were no conclusive matches, although Brandon's Hardware carries a large stock of yellow nylon rope and they did say that Jim Reynolds' face looked familiar and that they thought that he had been in the store, but nothing definite."

"Thank you, Constable."

The team was dismissed and Susan stayed behind to get her thoughts together. She was just about to pack up and go back to The Bayfield Village Inn for a swim when there was a knock on the door.

"Come in," Susan called out and Rose Blair entered.

"Oh, Susan, do you have a minute? I've got something to show you."

Rose took out the copy of the Sotheby's catalogue and spent the following twenty minutes showing Susan the Stewart-Barclays silverware and the dates of the auction sales.

"So you see these items never found themselves onto the cargo ship. Somehow they got left behind?"

"Thank you, Rose, this is so helpful. You said that Alice and Dave Bradbury live on Tuyl Street and that they have in their possession a silver tea service and a pair of candelabras? I think that I'll pay them a little visit."

Rose left the Lion's Hall and cycled home. When she got in Tom was waiting.

"Darling, Paul and Atsuko called. They have been staying in Toronto for a few days and now they're coming up tomorrow to visit us!"

"Oh, Tom, that's fantastic, I can hardly wait to see them. But why are they here?"

"They have two weeks holiday and they wanted to surprise everyone, plus the fact that they managed to find some last-minute deals on the air tickets."

"I'll go and make up the guest room. How wonderful. That's the best news I've had in ages."

Susan arrived at the Bradbury's house mid-afternoon. She had telephoned first to make sure that they would be in although Alice did say that they were due at the Croquet Club at five. She would make her visit brief.

Alice answered the door and Susan immediately liked her. She smiled broadly and was most welcoming.

"Do please come in. I've made some iced tea. Would you like a glass? Dave's in the garden, shall I call him in?"

"Oh, I don't think that will be necessary, Mrs. Bradbury."

"Please, dear, call me Alice."

"Well, Alice, I'm making enquiries about your silverware. When did you purchase your tea set and the candelabra?"

"Oh, we didn't buy them. They were a gift from our son, John."

"When did he give them to you?"

"Well, it was our 35th wedding anniversary. He said that it was a belated silver wedding anniversary present."

"And when was that?"

"Oh, it was in 2003."

"Would you mind showing me the pieces, Alice?"

"Why, certainly but could you tell me what this is all about?"

Susan took out the Sotheby's catalogue and showed the listed items which she had highlighted with a yellow pen.

"So, you see, Alice, we wondered how your son could afford to purchase these highly collectable 'one of a kind' pieces?"

"I don't understand. John said he bought them at a flea

market. Good God, he could never afford to pay this sort of money. That would be over $30,000, no way. These cannot be the same pieces, just good copies."

Alice showed Susan into the dining room and she studied the gleaming silverware before her on the sideboard.

"They are extremely beautiful. Now, the giveaway apparently is the Stewart-Barclays family crest embossed next to the Hallmark. Let's have a look."

They both peered intently at the underside of first the tea pot and then one of the candelabras. Sure enough, embossed in the silver was the crest alongside the Hallmark.

Alice frowned as she put the silver back on the sideboard.

"So, what exactly are you saying? Do you believe that John stole these? Surely not?"

"I'm not sure what's going on, Alice. As far as we knew this silver should have been at the bottom of the lake along with all the rest of the contents of the Stewart-Barclays cargo. How it should end up at Sotheby's and how your son could afford to buy it we have yet to discover. We will have to have a talk with him. I'm sure that there is a very simple explanation for all of this."

Susan felt bad. So often in her job she had to be the harbinger of bad news. Alice seemed one of those genuinely nice people who didn't deserve to have a rotten son. She sighed as she waved goodbye and drove back to the Lion's Hall to pick up Sergeant Flowers. They were going to drive to Cambridge to have that little talk with John Bradbury.

Before Susan set off for Cambridge, she decided to make a phone call to Sotheby's. She wanted to just confirm that John Bradbury had indeed purchased the silverware from the auction house. Sotheby's at first would not disclose the purchaser. They had a privacy agreement with all their clients but when Susan explained that she was with the Serious Crimes Unit, they obligingly gave her all the information that she needed and it was not what she had been expecting.

There had been a few pieces of the Stewart-Barclay silver that had not reached the reserve price, namely, the silver tea set and two candelabras. When Susan had asked who the client was, Sotheby's again hesitated. She had to remind them that her enquiry was all part of an ongoing murder investigation. They finally complied and released the name of the man who had put the Stewart-Barclays silver up for auction.

To Susan's horror it was none other than Jim Reynolds.

Jim Reynolds and John Bradbury were obviously inexplicably involved in the whole case, murder and all.

After Tom had told her about Paul and Atsuko's impending visit, Rose went into overdrive. They had not seen Paul for two years and she wanted to make his visit as wonderful and memorable as possible. As usual when stressed, Rose turned to baking. First, she made Paul's favourite cake, chocolate and cranberry torte, then she made a batch of raisin oatmeal cookies, an apple pie, and a large tray of carrot and walnut muffins.

When that was done she made a pot of tea and sat down at her computer. Lena had sent her the final draft map of the *Shipwrecks of the Great Storm of 1913*, and Rose perused this carefully. Lena had also included the estimated latitude and longitude and the GPS coordinates of the lost ships.

Rose looked very carefully at the cross marking where the Hydrus had gone down. How could all the cargo disappear with the boat, yet some of the Stewart-Barclays silver resurface almost one hundred years later? The only answer could be that the silver was never on the ship in the first place or that divers had already found the lost cargo and removed it from the boat?

She fished out the copy of the ship's manifest and again studied it intently. If the Stewart-Barclays cargo was not aboard the ship, then where on earth was it and who would have the answers? Who stood to inherit their wealth on their death?

Rose thought back to the history lesson from John Bradbury and she remembered that the Stewart-Barclays had died intestate. The next of kin would be Richard Stewart-Barclay's brother or, Rose presumed, Sophia's sister in Kincardine.

But why would their cargo not be aboard the ship in the first place? Rose shook her head, closed her computer firmly and told herself, enough thinking about the past. She had much more important things to do now in the present. After all, their darling son was coming home for a visit.

EIGHTEEN

S usan gathered the team together and, without any preamble she welcomed them all. "Good morning everyone. Let's have your reports. First, Constable Mathieson, what did you find out in Kincardine?"

Constable Mathieson stood up and cleared his throat. He was not used to giving reports. Normally his partner Sergeant Flowers took the lead role.

"Yes, well, I did find Sophia Stewart-Barclay's sister's granddaughter, I suppose that would make her Sophia's great niece. Mind, it took some searching, but I finally tracked her down to a nursing home."

Susan looked up and asked.

"Not Malcolm Place nursing home?"

"No, ma'am, it was Huron Shore Retirement and Nursing Home. Hannah Ralpawnski, widow of Jan Ralpawnski, has been a resident of the nursing home for five years. She has some memory of her grandmother talking about her very rich sister, Sophia.

She recalls that not only were they extremely wealthy but

Richard Stewart-Barclay owned a whole stack of Imperial Oil bonds which she seemed to recall were never found in his bank or indeed anywhere after his death. People presumed that they somehow were lost along with the cargo when the ship went down. Hannah's grandmother did not receive a penny from the estate. It was all passed on to Richard Stewart-Barclay's brother in England.

That is all I have to report, ma'am."

"Thank you, Constable. Now, Constable Dailey any more results from showing the photographs around?"

"No, ma'am, nothing more to report on that front."

"Well, I have quite a lot to report." Susan said as she flicked through her notes on the laptop. "Firstly, the coroner's report is in for Sam Pierce. He was hit on the head with, what the coroner thinks, was a spade. That caused the cut on his head but did not kill him. When he was thrown down the well, his neck was broken along with several other bones in his body.

Now on to our visit to Cambridge! It was a bit abortive although John Bradbury's wife was more than helpful. They live on Laurel Street, off Eagle, just as you come into Cambridge, an upscale neighbourhood. When we arrived, John was supposed to be on his way back from work where he is a lecturer at the university.

His wife was expecting him and so she invited us in for a cup of coffee.

She was very open and friendly, told us that John was a friend of Jim Reynolds and that they had known each other for over ten years. Jim had apparently filled John in with some of the history of Kincardine as he had relatives living in that area.

She also told me that John was fascinated with the Great Storm of 1913 and had conducted a great deal of research into the lost ships. All of this information was volunteered over coffee. When her husband still had not arrived an hour later she telephoned the university as he was not responding to his cell phone.

She was told that he had left the building three hours ago. I left her with firm instructions to call me when he turned up."

Susan opened her briefcase and pulled out a piece of typed paper emailed to her from Sotheby's. She began to read from it.

"The other piece of information I have to report is pertaining to the Stewart-Barclay's silver. It was put up for auction at Sotheby's ten years ago by Jim Reynolds of Wingham. Some of the pieces did not reach the reserve prices listed and therefore did not sell.

These pieces were the tea set and the candelabras which somehow fell into John Bradbury's hands and ended up being given to his parents as an anniversary present.

The question to be answered is where did Jim Reynolds get the silver from in the first place and why John ended up with some of it?

So, gentlemen, Constable Mathieson, continue digging around in Kincardine, find out where the cargo was stored prior to being loaded aboard the ship and take another look at Sinclair and Sons and how they operated?

Sergeant Flowers, I want you at the university. Ask around and check out the good professor and then look into his bank accounts. Dailey, go back up to Tobermory and look through all the *Diva Diving* records. See if you can find anything connecting them to Jim Reynolds or John Bradbury."

Right, we have work to do. Meet back here at the same time tomorrow."

NINETEEN

Paul and Atsuko arrived just as Tom was watering the garden in the front of the house. Rose had been anxiously looking out of the window on and off for the past hour and the minute that she saw the car pull up she ran out to greet them.

"Oh, Paul, Atsuko, it's just so lovely to see you both again. Come and give me a hug."

Paul, six foot two and eyes of blue, handsome in a fresh faced, gangly way, jumped out of the car and hugged Rose lovingly. Atsuko, as pretty and petite as a Japanese painted doll, short black hair gleaming like jet black coal, eyes twinkling with happiness, gave Rose a more restrained hug. As she put her arms around her Rose noticed a diamond ring glittering on her slender finger.

'Oh, Paul, Atsuko, you're engaged!! You never told us. How wonderful. Congratulations, darlings."

Tom hugged both Paul and Atsuko and Ben jumped up tail wagging and joined in the family celebration. They all went into the house and Tom opened a bottle of wine to toast the newly engaged couple.

"So, mom, what's this all about scarecrows, bodies and shipwrecks? Anne said that you all had quite a scare last weekend. What on earth is going on?"

Atsuko and Paul had spent their first night in Toronto with Anne. She had met them at the airport and had taken them back to her apartment. Seth had temporarily moved out and wouldn't be back until after she had left for Halifax, which was just as well as Paul and Seth had never seen eye to eye.

"Well, darling, sleepy, old Bayfield has well and truly been woken up by some awful foul play and it's all tied up with the Great Storm of 1913. You know, I emailed you a couple of weeks ago and told you all about the Historical Society's contribution to the centenary commemoration plans. Actually, Lena just finished the map which we're hoping to sell to raise funds for the archives building. Would you like to see it?"

"Yes, mom, it all sounds fascinating."

Rose looked at her son and wondered if he was being sarcastic. She never knew with him but he actually looked quite serious. She pulled up the map on her computer and Paul leant over to study it intently.

"You know that both Atsuko and I got our scuba diving licenses last year when we were in Thailand.

I wouldn't mind diving for this ship, the Hydrus. Boy, it would be quite exciting. You said in your email that the cargo aboard the ship was worth a fortune. Well, why hasn't the ship been found and salvaged years ago?"

"There have been a number of attempts and they did find the Wexford in 2000, eighty-seven years after it had gone down, but so far, nobody has found the Hydrus. The two divers from Tobermory had supposedly come down to dive for the Hydrus and nobody knows if they found the ship.

There was a local man, Jeff Sinclair who had spent years trying to find the lost ships. Look, if you study the map both the Carruthers and the Hydrus, reputedly, went down just off the coast of Port Franks."

Paul and Atsuko studied the map again.

"Cool, this is so cool, mom. When can we dive?"

Rose smiled. Their son had always been the impulsive one of their three children. *An adventurer,* she thought as she put her laptop away and prepared to set the table for lunch. Maybe it would be fun for them to go diving. They would have to borrow some gear and, instead of Tom sailing them down to Port Franks, which took far too long, they could drive down and ask their friend Bernie if he would mind taking the kids out in his boat to dive.

It was ironic, she thought, that those lost ships had been silently resting on the bottom of Lake Huron for a hundred years undisturbed and as soon as Lena's map went public she was sure that there would be hundreds of divers, like Paul, eager to discover the lost ships. *Diva Diving School* could have been onto a thriving business, Rose thought sadly.

"Ok, everyone, lunch is ready and after we've eaten you two can go off and explore the village and maybe go to the beach while dad and I stay here. We'll have an early barbecue and then you young things can go and hit the nightlife of Bayfield. Well, at least go for a drink in The Black Dog or somewhere. Tomorrow, if Bernie is fine with it, we'll drive you both down to Port Franks and you can go diving. How is that for a plan?"

Paul kissed his mother and said: "It's just so great to be back, mom, I love it here."

They all sat down to a pleasant lunch and Rose thought how her family was the most important thing in the world.

Susan had arrived a little late for their briefing session. She had decided to swim one hundred lengths of the pool and hadn't realized the time; as a consequence, she arrived at the Lion's Hall with wet hair and a rather disheveled look.

It had not helped that she had gone to The Dock's the previous evening and had drunk one too many glasses of wine.

Even the swimming had not shaken off her fuzzy head. Boy, she hated hangovers.

"Right, good morning everyone. Let's be hearing from you all. First, Sergeant Flowers, any news on the professor?"

"I spent the afternoon at the university and spoke to a number of his colleagues. He appears to be well liked and his students all said positive things about him. The official reason for his absence according to the Faculty Head, was compassionate leave for a grandparent who had passed away. His wife knew nothing about this and when I checked with his parents, they told me that John's grandparents had passed away many years ago.

Alice said that she had spoken to her son after you, ma'am, had been around looking at their silver. We think that when he got wise to the fact that we were onto him he took off. We have sent out a description of his car, registration number and a photograph to all the police units across Ontario. Unless he headed across the border we will find him."

"Thank you, Sergeant. Now, Constable Mathieson, anything to report from Kincardine?"

"Yes ma'am. I found out where the ships' warehouses used to be but they are no longer standing, in fact a new subdivision has been built where they used to be. I got talking to some fishermen down by the docks and they gave me the name of a man who they reckoned his father had worked with on the Hydrus. I tracked him down eventually; he lives with his son now and is very frail, must be in his late eighties but still quite sharp. He says that his father often talked about a big scam that used to go on. Apparently, one of the sons of the Insurance company, Sinclair and Sons, had some sort of deal going on. He wasn't sure what, but he knows that his father knew about it and did not approve. That is all I have to report."

"Thank you, Constable. Now, Constable Dailey, did you find anything up in Tobermory?"

"Yes, ma'am, it was quite a serendipitous visit as Mrs. Richards was in the process of clearing out the *Diva Diving* offices. She was quite open to me helping her, and we made a number of interesting discoveries.

Firstly, among a pile of Lake charts we found an original shipping plan for the Hydrus.

Apparently all the registered cargo ships had defined routes that they had to follow and this chart, that was found, showed the Hydrus's route quite clearly. Ian and Sam had highlighted where they must have thought the boat went down off the coast of Port Franks.

Secondly, we found an email from Jim Reynolds suggesting that they meet in Bayfield to discuss a business arrangement.

We could find no communications from John Bradbury.

Mrs. Richards did say that Ian and Sam had become quite excited at the prospect of what was called shipwreck hunting.

They had been quite successful in Georgian Bay, had discovered a number of sunken boats but had not found any treasure yet. She was under the impression that the guys thought that they were onto the 'big one' with the Hydrus."

Susan thought for a minute.

"Right, this is how I see it. Somehow, somewhere the Stewart-Barclay's cargo got stashed away and never made it on the ship. So we now have the Hydrus sailing with an empty hold. Surely the crew would know that the containers were empty unless they had been substituted for something else?

The manifest, however, clearly stated the Stewart-Barclay's cargo as being the only cargo aboard the ship when it left Kincardine on November 8th, 1913. We know that silver pieces came up for auction in 2003 and somehow found their way into John Bradbury's hands, although Jim Reynolds was the vendor.

We also know that the treasure seekers, Ian and Sam, were last seen alive in Bayfield. Then there is the grandson of Sinclair and Son's also searching for lost ships. Gentlemen, we have a number of loose ends to tie up but we are very close to solving this case. Sergeant Flowers, we must find John Bradbury. Get onto that immediately. Constable Mathieson, go back to Kincardine and see if you can uncover this scam. Constable Dailey, go back to Wingham and see what you can discover there. Get a search warrant to search Jim Reynolds house and computer. Right, go to it men, bring me back some positive results."

Bernie had agreed to take Paul and Atsuko out on his boat but he had laughed when they told him that they wanted to dive for the Hydrus.

"You'll be lucky, my lad, to find it. It will be like looking for a needle in a haystack, the lake is huge. Besides, rumour has it that the Hydrus went down much further north."

"Well, mom is convinced that the ship is here somewhere

and so we'll give it our best. It will be fun to dive in Lake Huron.

Atsuko and I haven't had time to do much diving, so this is a great opportunity for us."

They boarded his boat with some scuba diving equipment that Rose had managed to borrow from her friend Cathy.

It was a perfect day for sailing. The lake was calm but there was a hint of a breeze which fanned out the sails sufficiently to move the boat along at a good four knots.

"So, where do we go from here?" Bernie asked with a bemused look on his face.

"Well, these are the coordinates and this is the record of the wind speeds during the storm. Dad and I calculated that with winds over 80mph the Hydrus could have ended up just about here."

Paul pointed to the map on his lap. Tom had spent a good hour pouring over the map with him doing calculations, trying to work out the drift speed of the boat.

"We could do with some fancy sonar equipment. Do you know that the 'Wexford' was actually found by a fisherman called Don Chalmers? He couldn't understand why his fishing nets kept getting snagged plus his 'fish-finder' kept showing anomalies.

He was N.W. of Grand Bend when his 'fish-finder' distinctly showed the contour of the hull of a ship. Shipwreck hunters, David Trotter and Robin Wilson, came in with their 'electronic fish', a two-meter steel tornado full of electrical sonar equipment, and using that they found the Wexford sitting upright on the bottom of the Lake.

It was encrusted with Zebra mussels. Anyway, my lad, best of luck finding the boat. It would be great if you did, but don't get your hopes up too high."

Paul and Atsuko looked back at the shoreline which was lined with huge sand dunes. Port Franks could never have protected any ships in the Great Storm; there just was no proper harbour, least of all a sheltered one.

The lake was positively dancing with light sparkling off the water which was a beautiful turquoise blue. *Oh, it was so good to be back in Huron County and to be sailing on Lake Huron,* Paul thought as they headed out into deep water.

"Right, according to the GPS we're pretty close to the coordinates that I entered. Can you stop the boat now, Bernie, thank you? Atsuko, we should get ready for our dive."

Looking down into the water it appeared crystal clear. *Could the Hydrus really be down there* Paul thought as he clipped on his mask and tested the oxygen bottles.

Atsuko and Paul made five dives all into different locations. They were about to call it a day when Paul noticed a large rock-like shadow appearing at the bottom of the lake. Swimming closer he realized that he was looking at the hull of a boat submerged deeply in the sand and covered in Zebra Mussels.

Where the cargo and cabin area should have been was just an empty shell.

Scattered across the sandy bottom of the lake were objects identified only by their shape as everything was encrusted in Zebra Mussels; there were chairs, tables, kitchen utensils. The deck rails were mangled and the porthole glass smashed, although in a few instances, panes of glass still appeared intact.

Paul had no idea if it was indeed the Hydrus but given the coordinates and the approximate size of the boat, he felt that it was a strong possibility that they were actually looking at the long, lost boat. He signaled to Atsuko that they should ascend.

"We found it, Bernie; I think that we have actually found it," Paul shouted as soon as he had broken the surface. Atsuko followed, and both were soon aboard the boat and headed back to Port Franks.

Back in Bayfield they couldn't wait to tell Rose and Tom their news but when they arrived home, there was only Tom around.

"Where's mom?" Paul sounded just like the little boy he once was, always a 'mummy's' boy continually wanting to know the whereabouts of his mother.

"She had to go around to her friend Alice's house. Their son, John, has been killed in a car accident and as soon as she heard the news she rushed out."

"Not John, as in the history professor, who mom thought had something to do with the silver and the lost ship's cargo?"

"Yes, Paul, the police wanted to question him and he took off. I'm afraid that your mother feels partially responsible for his death."

"Oh, poor mom! Well, that's rather burst our bubble, dad. We think that we've found the Hydrus, well at least it was close to where we calculated that it might be. Unfortunately, we couldn't stay down too long as Atsuko was getting pretty tired, in fact, she's really beat. Would it be ok if she lies down for a bit? I think that we are both also somewhat jet lagged."

"Certainly, both of you should go for a nap. I'll wake you in time for dinner."

Atsuko smiled tiredly, nodded her pretty head, and padded after Paul. She had barely spoken a word to either Tom or Rose since their arrival.

Oh, how I hate this part of my job, Susan thought as she broke the news of their son's death to Alice and Dave. Such good people didn't deserve such tragedy in their lives.

Of course, the fact that John had been in a police chase when his car overturned was another matter, and Susan was going to try to keep that part of his death away from his parents for the time being.

They didn't want to hear that their son was a criminal, no, not when they were trying to deal with the trauma of his death.

Susan had called Rose and asked if she could come to sit with Alice and Dave. They would need the love and support of their friends to get them through this ghastly time. At least, they had not been called to identify the body. John's wife had that gruesome task.

But, on a purely business note, Susan wondered where John's death left them with their enquiry?

Unless they traced Jim, they still had far too many unanswered questions.

Hopefully, the team would come up with some of the answers, but she had really been pinning her hopes on interviewing John.

Rose arrived and Susan could see that she looked a little tearful.

The whole investigation had been hard on her friend who seemed to have unwittingly been pulled into the case like a pawn on a chess board. She left Alice, Dave, and Rose and returned to the Lion's Hall.

Rose returned home to Bayfield Terrace feeling thoroughly washed out. She couldn't stop beating herself up.

If only she hadn't got involved in all the research into the lost ships; if only she hadn't noticed Alice and Dave's silver, if only she hadn't contacted Sotheby's.

Too many, if onlys, and Rose was not normally the sort of person that lived with regrets. That day though, she was flooded with mixed emotions and the only positive thing that kept her going was the thought of seeing Paul and his lovely fiancé Atsuko, and of course, Tom. They were the light in her darkness.

When she arrived home, the house was dead quiet. Tom was watching his beloved football and there was no sign of either Paul or Atsuko.

There was, however, the most divine smell wafting through from the kitchen. Tom, bless his soul, had cooked dinner.

"Hi, I'm home darling. What's cooking? It smells divine!"

"Oh, I've made a beef casserole; it should be ready in about thirty minutes. Paul and Atsuko have gone for a little nap. They're really bushed after their dive. But, love, it looks as if they found the Hydrus. I'll let Paul tell you himself when he wakes up."

"Wow, I can hardly believe that after one hundred years they've actually found the boat! That's almost a miracle. Gosh, that is good news.

Oh but Tom, I feel so bad. If I hadn't gotten involved with all that history on the Stewart-Barclays, I would never have known about the silver and John would still be alive. I feel as if it's entirely my fault."

Big, glistening tears started to well up in Rose's eyes and Tom drew her to him to comfort her.

"Of course it's not your fault, love, John was into something no good otherwise he would never have been running from the police."

Paul interrupted them by appearing in the kitchen.

"Hi Mom, gosh, something smells great. Actually, I'm starving. You'll never guess what, we found the lost ship, at least we think that it's your ship the Hydrus something?"

"Did you find the cargo?"

"Not really, there was really very little around other than what looked like standard ship stuff and everything was encrusted in Zebra Mussels. Didn't I see on the manifest that there was even a grand piano and all sorts of furniture in the cargo? Well, I think that I would have recognised a grand piano even one covered in Zebra Mussels. I think that you should contact the police and let them send in their own divers down to check the boat out."

"You're right, Paul, I'll call Susan now and then we'll open a bottle of wine and toast your success."

In the space of thirty minutes Susan received two very important phone calls.

One was from Rose who told her the amazing news that her son had discovered the lost ship which in theory had been carrying the Stewart-Barclays cargo.

The second call came from the Bureau of Serious Crimes in Montreal, Quebec. Jim Reynolds' haulage business had been on their radar for over a year and when they saw his name listed on the Ontario Most Wanted, they knew that something was up.

Susan was to meet with Inspector Henri Le Bruin the following day.

Curiouser and curiouser, thought Susan as she sat down to eat her dinner, this time at DaVinci's Restaurant, a huge lasagna, and a Caesar salad, accompanied by a large glass of wine.

The case was definitely heating up.

TWENTY

The team arrived earlier than usual as Susan wanted to finish their briefing and be able to arrive in London on time to pick Inspector Henri Le Bruin up from the airport. They had a meeting scheduled at the Head Office with the Chief Superintendent.

"Right, who wants to go first and remember, time is of the essence, I must be away by ten, no later. I see Dailey. You look keen to go first. What have you to report?"

"I obtained a search warrant and took away Jim Reynolds' computer. Our computer guys found much of interest, and I think that you're going to like this. Our Jimmy boy..."

Susan flinched as the Constable called him that and at the same time she wondered just what they had found on the computer. Had she ever emailed him?

She couldn't remember but felt quite nervous at the thought. Constable Dailey continued....

"Our Jimmy boy it seems has been running two separate operations both of which originated with his father, James Sinclair.

Both businesses were connected to haulage. One business appears quite legit, that's the one that is going belly up into receivership, but the other operation that he has kept very much under wraps, is thriving if his bank account is anything to go by.

It appears that he has been part of a huge syndicate hauling stolen goods, mostly fine art from Ontario up to Montreal where it is shipped off to buyers from all over the world.

Now we're not dealing in small numbers here, we've been looking at millions of dollar's worth of artwork being transported up the 401 at least six times a year. Constable Daily referred to his notebook before continuing.

"We have an address in Verdun, a warehouse by the looks of things. We also have a few names, one of which, ma'am, you will find extremely interesting, Roy LeRoy. Remember 2008 that art heist at the McMichael Art Gallery in Kleinberg and how we almost nailed him, but he did a runner just before we could bring him in? Well, his name is connected to Jim Reynolds, and he appears to be on his payroll.

Constable Dailey opened a brown envelope he had retrieved from a briefcase sitting on the floor by the table. He pulled out a sheaf of papers and held them in his hand. "In his office safe, we found these very old Imperial Oil bonds. Look, they are made out to a Richard Stewart-Barclay and were issued by Jake Englehart, Vice President of Imperial Oil, dated 1896.

Also in his safe we found copies of the Stewart-Barclay's last will and testament.

It appears that they left all their worldly goods to Mrs. Stewart-Barclay's sister in Kincardine. Amongst other things we discovered a ledger book which must date back to when

Jim's father first started his haulage business. Look; the first date entered was 1912.

This ledger records artwork received by some very famous artists. He passed the ledger around so that the team could all have a look at the contents.

"There are names of French Impressionists, quite a few Groups of Seven pieces and some of Emily Carr's paintings, then later on there are some of Salvador Dali's work, some Georgia O'Keeffe, even a couple of Picasso's.

I seem to recall that the Stewart-Barclays owned a number of the Group of Seven paintings.

Anyway, we have uncovered enough evidence here to implicate Jim Reynolds to an international syndicate based out of Montreal. I think that Interpol might be very interested in our man Jim."

Constable Dailey sat down with a big smile on his face. He was beginning to enjoy himself.

"Thank you, Constable; you certainly uncovered an unprecedented amount of evidence, well done. Now, Mathieson, what have you to report from Kincardine?"

"I went back to the old man, a Mr. McEachern, and prodded a bit more. He said that his father worked for James Sinclair in the years before he set up the haulage business when he was still part of Sinclair and Sons before the war. This was of course when Sinclair and Sons were at their peak of being underwriters to Lloyd's of London and the local shipping agent too.

Mr. McEachern told me that his father always said that young James Sinclair was a wily, scheming fox and that he was stealing goods from right under his father's nose.

This James Sinclair apparently had the crew of the

Hydrus on his payroll. When it came to loading the cargo onto the ship, the crew would switch the cargo and substitute it with grain.

When the cargo arrived at its destination and the grain was found, they would say that a mistake had been made. Of course, the real cargo was never discovered and, in many cases, the stolen art works were never reported missing, probably because the owners had procured them by dubious means in the first place.

Anyway, Mr. McEachern gave me an address of where he thought James Sinclair had his warehouse.

I checked this out and sure enough, up until 1950, there had been a warehouse, apparently tucked behind Coombe's Furniture Factory, but that is long since gone and there is now a coffee shop in its place. That's about all that I have, ma'am."

"Thank you, Constable. Sergeant Flowers, did you manage to look at John Bradbury's bank account?"

"Yes, he has been receiving a lump sum of $20,000 a year from Jim Reynolds for the past ten years. His wife has no knowledge of this money or where it came from.

She does remember John being particularly excited ten years ago, and when questioned, he told her that he had a little business transaction going on with a man from Wingham.

I asked if I could look at his study and I found all sorts of research material on Kincardine, particularly, a whole section on the history of Sinclair and Sons.

In fact, he seemed almost obsessive about them even tracing their family tree. There were diagrams charting the Sinclair family since their arrival in Kincardine in 1848 right up to present day including our Jim 'Sinclair' Reynolds."

"Sergeant, do you have any evidence that indicates that John Bradbury knew what Jim Reynolds was up to?"

"Well, yes and no, ma'am! In amongst John's university papers, we found a copy of the deeds of the original warehouse in Kincardine where Jim's father stored the stolen cargo. Now how much John knew and how much he guessed that we don't know, but it was obvious that John was onto something."

"Thank you, sergeant. Gentlemen, it looks as if we are closing in on Jim Reynolds. Let me summarize what we know to date. James Sinclair, way back in 1912, was working an insurance fraud filtering off pieces of fine art from select cargo and finding suitable buyers. His son, Jim, continued this illegal business but took it to a far different level. He established an international business shipping artworks through a cartel in Montreal to Europe and Asia. Now this is the bit that gets a bit murky for us. About ten years ago, if we go by the Sotheby's auction and John Bradbury's first payment of $20,000 we can surmise that John must have uncovered Jim's scam. At the time John was researching the history of Kincardine and I suspect that he found out about the warehouse which was used to store the stolen goods. Also, I suspect that he confronted Jim, having tracked him down to Wingham, and probably started to blackmail him. He maybe was fobbed off with the Stewart-Barclay's silver to begin with and then got greedy and demanded $20,000 a year as a payoff to keep quiet. Until we apprehend Jim, we will not know the details."

Susan paused to take a breath and to inwardly sigh. To think that she was in love with the man made her shudder deep inside. She braced herself and continued with the summary.

"As to our luckless shipwreck hunters, Ian and Sam and also Jeff Sinclair, they were getting very close to discovering that there was indeed no cargo aboard the Hydrus, and if that was revealed, the whole fraudulent scheme would blow up in

Jim's face. Don't forget that we are talking about major stakes here; Jim was playing with the big boys and dealing in millions of dollars' worth of stolen goods. I suspect that Jim was probably in over his head. You don't associate with the Montreal mobsters without getting into real deep waters. No, Ian, Sam, and Jeff were killed by either John or Jim."

Susan went quiet allowing the team to digest the information. She continued talking but with a quieter tone of voice. "Now, I had a phone call from Rose Blair. Her son, Paul went diving off the coast of Port Franks and found the Hydrus. From what he could see there was little evidence of any cargo. We have the GPS coordinates and a team of police divers are down there as we speak. We will know more by tomorrow which, incidentally, is our last day here in the Lion's Hall and in Bayfield, so after our debriefing tomorrow the drinks are on me at The Albion. OK, now I must go to London. I expect full reports on my desk ready to send to the Head Office tomorrow. Great work, everyone."

Susan hastily packed up her papers, put her laptop in her bag, grabbed her purse, and car keys and left the building at top speed. She would be horribly late if she did not hurry.

Inspector Henri Le Bruin was in his fifties, a youthful looking man with a very European flair about him. *He's probably a first-generation immigrant* Susan thought as she shook his hand and introduced herself.

She had arrived at London airport in time to grab a quick cup of coffee from the airport's Tim Hortons, all before the Inspector walked through the Arrivals door.

Henri had a slight look of George Clooney about him; salt and pepper hair which ten years ago would have been jet black and piercing, dark, liquid, brown eyes. He was slim in build, well dressed in a shabby-chic manner. No suit and tie for this Inspector. Instead he wore khaki pants and a crisp, white shirt with the sleeves rolled up to his elbows. He carried a black leather satchel over his shoulder.

"Bonjour, Inspector Parker, comment ça va?"

"*Ça va bien*, oh but please say that you can speak English because my French is awful?"

"Of course I speak English, I was just testing you."

Henri laughed, and as he spoke Susan felt a warm fuzzy feeling infuse her body, chemistry that signaled an attraction to the opposite sex.

This was one man that I would like to get to know more intimately, Susan thought. Maybe it was just the sexy French accent, but she certainly felt a strong attraction.

They drove to the Serious Crimes Headquarters on Richmond and were ushered into the Chief's office. After formal introductions Henri immediately got down to business. He opened his satchel and pulled out his laptop and then proceeded to show them pictures of haulage trucks going up and down the 401.

He then homed in on one particular truck which bore the name of Sinclair Haulage on the side.

"These are just a few of the hundreds of photographs that we have of Sinclair's Haulage trucks going up and down the 401. We have been staking out this particular firm for many years, since one of their trucks was caught on a security camera off-loading artwork. Unfortunately, when we raided the haulage firm in Wingham, Jim Reynolds flatly denied that his firm had any business in Montreal. When we checked the license plates on the camera footage, the registration number did not match Jim Reynolds truck.

We have continued to have his firm under surveillance, but the man is like a slippery eel, very difficult to catch.

But one thing is for sure and that is the Montreal Mobsters are involved, and this Jim is well and truly in deep waters. They are sharks and they will eat him alive. Now, you say that Jim Reynolds is wanted for murder? Can you fill me in with your side of the investigation, *s'il vous plaît?*"

Susan proceeded to tell the Inspector all that her team had put together concluding with the fact that Jim Reynolds was still on the run.

"I hate to say, Inspector, but our man could be anywhere in the world by now. All he had to do was get on a plane to Europe, then he would literally just be able to disappear. I'm sure that he has been siphoning off money to various banks accounts, he would be under the radar. No, even though we have Interpol alerted, mon Dieu, this man could easily have escaped."

Susan sighed as the meeting wrapped up. In crime novels the criminals always got caught but not in real life. They had files and files of cold cases, some of which she knew would never be solved.

Susan was about to leave the room when she was tapped on the shoulder. Turning, she found Henri Le Bruin standing next to her with a sexy smile on his handsome face.

"Inspector Susan, would you like to join me for dinner? I'm all alone in this wonderful city and a man should never be alone when there's a beautiful woman nearby."

What a smooth talker, Susan thought. What the heck, a girl has to do what a girl has to do, and she smiled broadly as she accepted Henri's invitation.

TWENTY-ONE

TWO WEEKS LATER

R ose and Tom had a wonderful fortnight with Paul and Atsuko. Rose did not visit the archives building once during their stay and she promised Tom that she would cut back on her volunteering.

Just before Paul and Atsuko were about to depart, Paul announced that they would like to get married in Bayfield the following July. Rose was positively amazed.

"But, what about Atsuko's family? Surely they will want her to be married in Japan?"

"Oh, Mom, of course we will be married in Japan, but it is very common there to have several weddings and the bride gets to wear different wedding dresses to each one including the traditional Japanese kimono.

No, we would have the Japanese wedding and then come to Bayfield for a Canadian wedding. I think it's cool."

"Where will you have the wedding, darling?"

"At the Town Hall, where else? it's so pretty and Atsuko thinks that it is like something out of Anne of Green Gables. We're going to Prince Edward Island for our honeymoon."

"Talking of vacations, your father and I have booked a holiday to Austria and we leave next week. We're going to stay in a castle in Vienna, one owned once by William McGarvey from Petrolia from just down the road in Lambton County." Seeing the blank expression on Paul's face she added. "He was an oil baron, over one hundred years ago."

"Mom, there you go again with your history. Don't you ever stop thinking about the past?"

"Well, my darling, the present is shaped by what happened in the past just as the future depends on the present, you cannot really separate them. Yes, I know it can be boring listening to your mother talk on about history but it's only because it fascinates me so.

You know that every small community in Canada has quite amazing stories to tell about their ancestors who came from all over the world looking for a better life.

Some of those early pioneers had a horrendous time.

In the winters, they almost froze to death and in the summers, when Huron County was nothing but trees and swamps, people died of malaria.

No, we are so lucky to be living in our comfortable world. Enough of that! Paul, Atsuko, promise me that you will always be kind to each other, oh and love each other my darlings, love is all that it takes. Now give your old mother a kiss before I start crying."

"Oh, mom, why are you crying?"

"Darlings, I know how much I'm going to miss you; Japan is just so far away."

"But you will be coming to the wedding, I mean the Japanese one?"

"Your father and I wouldn't miss it for the world and we will make sure that you have a fabulous Canadian wedding here in Bayfield. Now you two need to get packing. You might need an extra suitcase with all the shopping that Atsuko did in the village."

Paul and Atsuko left the following morning.

To take her mind off their departure Rose cycled to the archives to tie up some loose ends before they flew to Austria. When she arrived, Lena rushed out of the archives building to greet her. "Rose, we haven't seen you for ages. Look, ta-da! The finished map. How do you like it?"

Rose studied the beautiful sepia toned gold tinted map before her. It was magnificent! Her eyes sought out the cross marking where the Hydrus had gone down.

"The only trouble is, Lena, we now only have one lost ship. The Hydrus has officially been notified as found. If nothing else, having both the Wexford and now the Hydrus so close, this surely will promote a bit of tourism in Huron County. Well, at least for those who like diving."

Lena listened carefully and then smiled saying; "Rose, I'd like to present you with this framed copy of the map. It will remind you of all the work that you put into The Great Storm of 1913."

"Thank you, Lena, that is so thoughtful of you, but to be honest, I'm beginning to wish that I had never started this research. It uncovered a trail of tragedy and death to a bunch of unsuspecting people.

First those poor sailors who lost their lives in the storm and the families whose lives were impacted by it and then more recently those divers from Tobermory. What a waste of young lives."

Rose packed up her laptop and was about to leave the

archives building when Angela came rushing over from the library,

"Oh, there you are Rose, I've got a delivery for you; the florist couldn't find anyone at your home so they delivered them here. I'm so glad you called in today. Here you are."

Angela handed Rose a beautiful bouquet of long-stemmed roses. On the little card was written.

Roses for my dear friend, Rose! Thank you for everything. We will get together again soon. When I get back from Montreal, I'll give you a call.

Your friend,

Susan

Rose smiled and, putting the flowers carefully in the basket at the front of her bicycle, she cycled back home.

———

THE NEXT ROSE BLAIR MYSTERY can be found HERE!

EPILOGUE

"Tom, this city is magnificent. Gosh, there is so much history. Oh, I'm already in love with it and we've only been here two days."

Rose and Tom had arrived in Vienna after an eight-hour flight from Toronto. As the plane had come into land, they could see the city beneath them extending across the lazy waters of the Danube.

Vienna was the capital, economic, and cultural centre of Austria. The palaces, parks, churches, and the grand residences made Vienna one of Europe's grandest cities.

On their first day, Rose and Tom visited St. Stephen's Cathedral which was initially designed in 1147 but not completed until the 16th century over four hundred years later.

Rose remembered reading a book by Ken Follett, "World Without End", a trilogy spanning three hundred years which followed the lives of the architects who were building a similar cathedral in England.

That first day, they visited the Vienna State Opera House, built in the 1860s, and for many years the centre of the city's cultural life as was the Burg Théâtre, the national theatre of Austria, which was situated just opposite the Rathaus or city hall.

On the second day, Rose and Tom explored the Schonbrunn Palace just 5km. from the city centre. This was built in 1750 for the Hapsburgs and apparently Napoleon Bonaparte lived there during his stay in Vienna.

They then took a tram down the main thoroughfare past large departmental stores with names which were recognizable throughout the world. There was The Gap, Bata Shoes, Marks & Spencer's, and the ever-present McDonalds and KFC along with Starbucks and Pizza Hut. Rose thought it a shame that everything was now so globalized.

After an hour of sightseeing on the tram they got off. Being or acting like tourists wasn't really Rose and Tom's style. One day of being a slave to the guidebook was enough. Tom took Rose's hand and said:

"Love, I've had enough of looking at tourist sights, let's just follow our noses and see where they take us."

Walking hand in hand down the cobbled streets of Vienna, down through little alleyways, past tiny squares with the prettiest of parks nestled with trees and benches, beautiful buildings, tree-lined boulevards, tramways crisscrossing the city, fountains and statues everywhere. How could one city be so intrinsically beautiful, yet harbor such a dark and tortured history?

Running to catch another tram, Rose laughed. She felt like a teenager again. This holiday had done wonders to restore her bruised soul.

"Tom, look, that's the Kartnerstrasse." Rose pointed to a long street shut off to traffic and filled with colourful cafés, umbrellas and awnings competing with each other for attention. The street was positively bustling with people.

"Can we get off here, Tom? I remember Susan telling me that this was one of her favourite places to visit when she came to Vienna last spring."

Tom and Rose jumped off the tram and pushed their way through the crowds, jostling to window shop or to find a suitable café to sit and watch the world go by.

The café Tom and Rose finally chose was tucked down a dark alleyway. There were barrels of geraniums stacked each side of the door and a red and white awning which had covered a large area of the sidewalk before it had been pedestrianized.

As they walked in, the bell on the door tingled, and a smartly dressed waiter appeared. In perfect English he said, "Will you be taking lunch?"

Rose replied, "Would it be alright if we just had coffee and dessert?"

"Certainly, madam!" And he pointed to a glass cabinet displaying a wonderful array of the most delicious cakes and patisseries.

"Shall we sit outside or inside?"

"It's much cooler inside, let's sit over here," Tom said. The waiter led them to a pretty circular table covered in a crisp, white cloth.

Hanging from the ceiling an amber glass lantern casting a soft, golden glow. In the middle of the table was a posy of fresh-cut flowers.

The restaurant appeared to be almost empty but Rose

could hear a couple talking quietly in the background. The sounds of a band playing a Viennese Waltz drifted through the open door.

There was a quiet settling across the city, a mid-afternoon lull between the bustling of lunch and the late evening reverie still to come. A gentle breeze stirred the air causing the lamp to sway slowly.

Rose and Tom sat down. The waiter stood attentively, notepad in hand ready to take their orders.

"Madam, would you like to choose from the cabinet? Can I get you a piece of our strudel or gateau or would you like me to bring your coffees first while you decide?"

Tom ordered an espresso and Rose a café latte. They chatted for a while and when the waiter returned, he asked if they had decided on their choice of dessert.

Rose could see a wonderful selection of pastries but at the back of the cabinet was a magnificent Black Forest Gateau lavishly covered with cream and great chunks of chocolate crowned with glistening, black cherries.

"I just have to have a piece of that Black Forest Gateau. What are you going to have, Tom?"

Tom stood up to get a better view of the display of desserts and as he did so Rose caught sight of the couple deep in conversation sitting at the next table.

She was just about to turn away to speak to Tom when out of the corner of her eye she noticed something familiar about the shape of the head of the older man still deep in conversation with a much younger woman.

At first glance Rose thought that the woman looked like Susan.

At that moment the waiter dropped a plate, the couple

looked up and Rose could clearly see that it wasn't Susan, but she immediately recognized the face of the man.

It was Jim.

KEEP READING for a sneak peek at the next Rose Blair Murder Mystery! Preorder HERE!

ACKNOWLEDGMENTS

Whilst this novel contains many historical facts pertaining to the Great Storm of 1913, all characters and the story line are a work of fiction.

Any errors and omissions of a historical or factual nature are mine and for this I humbly apologize.

I would like to thank my friends who read and edited, in particular Rita, who was my 'comma' advisor, and my husband for his support and patience during the process of writing this, my first full-length novel.

"Tom, Tom, wake up," Rose said as she elbowed her husband gently in his ribs. "It's seven thirty and isn't Doug picking you up at eight?"

Tom grunted and rolled over. As Rose got out of bed and pulled open the blinds the bright sun bathed their bedroom in lightness so much so that Tom buried his face under the duvet to stop the sun from blinding him.

It was a beautiful August morning and the garden looked particularly charming in the early sun. Rose walked out of their bedroom and padded down the hallway to their kitchen where she filled the kettle with water and prepared to make a pot of tea. It was blissfully quiet and for once the house was empty apart from Tom, herself, and, of course, Ben their faithful black Labrador. Thinking of Ben, Rose wondered where their beloved dog had gone. *Normally he wanted to go outside first thing in the morning, so where was he?*

It was then that Rose noticed that the back door was open, and just as she was registering this Ben came charging in jumping up to give her a big, wet lick. He then ran off to the bedroom to jump on the bed.

That will wake Tom up, Rose thought as she closed the back door. *But who had let Ben out in the first place?* A chill of fear ran down her spine as memories of the previous summer came flooding back. The scarecrow hanging from the pear tree had looked so real then, Rose would never forget the whole affair, ever.

She poured out two cups of tea and proceeded to carry them into the bedroom where Tom was now lying wide awake with Ben at his side.

"Here you are, love. Don't forget that you have a game of golf with Doug this morning. Oh, by the way, did you let Ben out into the garden?"

Tom sat bolt upright and glanced at the bedside clock saying, "Goodness, it's almost 8 o'clock. Doug will be here any minute now." With that he leapt out of bed and disappeared into the bathroom. Rose could hear the tap water running as Tom quickly brushed his teeth and threw on his clothes.

As if on cue, the doorbell rang. It was Doug, punctual as ever. Rose handed him a cup of tea and told him that Tom would be out shortly.

"Doug, you didn't come by earlier and let Ben out, did you?"

"I could hardly come into your house, Rose, as the front door was locked. Why the serious face?"

"Well...oh, it doesn't matter, I'm sure that there is a perfectly simple explanation. Oh, here is Tom. Have a good game you two. See you this afternoon."

Tom kissed Rose goodbye and the two men left, leaving Rose drinking her morning cup of tea. No sooner had they departed when the telephone rang.

"Oh, hi Mary...Oh my gosh. I completely forgot, yes, I'm still coming, just might be a little late. Just go ahead and practice without me. I'll be along in about 20 minutes."

Rose put the phone down and looked at the clock. *Why is it*, she thought for the umpteenth time, *why is it that we are so dictated to by the clock.* However, it had been her own fault for forgetting that she had planned to meet her friend Mary at the croquet courts at 8:00am. They both had wanted to get a practice in before their game at 8:45. It was now 8:15 and there she still was, in her dressing gown.

Mary had joined the Croquet Club the same time as Tom and her. Whereas Tom had mastered the game quickly, Rose had struggled with getting control of her mallet. In fact, Mary and she were as bad as each other, or as good, which is what Mary always said, "We're as good as each other," and Rose had thought to herself, *yes, we are good for each other*.

Mary had only moved to the village of Bayfield less than a year ago and they had met each other at fitness class. She was a little younger than Rose, small and wiry with eyes that twinkled like diamonds and a smile that would warm the coldest of winter mornings. They had instantly become the best of friends.

Indeed, it was Mary who had helped Rose make the canapés for Paul and Atsuko's wedding.

They had made little cucumber cups filled with an assortment of fillings, fig phyllo pastries, goats cheese tarts, cream cheese stuffed strawberries, fruit kebabs, bacon wrapped chestnuts, tiny blinis with smoked salmon and cream cheese, and the list went on. They had had such fun together, giggling like schoolgirls when several of the guests had asked for the name of the caterer.

That was back in June and now it was August, and Rose

only had Jessica and the girls left to visit one more time before the Labour Day weekend and the beginning of another school year.

Putting on her white three-quarter length pants and white short sleeved top, Rose grabbed her sun hat from the lobby cupboard. Although it was early in the morning, by nine the August sun would be beating down on their heads. She grabbed a water bottle and a little bag of orange and cranberry scones that she had baked the night before.

Mary didn't like baking, although, she was an excellent cook. Rose always baked too many muffins or scones and had got into the habit of bagging up surplus goodies to give to Mary.

Right, everything is ready, Rose thought, *I should get to the Croquet Club in time for a bit of a practice before the game. I must lock the front and back doors before I leave.*

Ever since the burglary the previous year, Rose had tried her hardest to remember to lock up the house before she left.

Her friend, Susan Parker, the Inspector, had really reprimanded her for not locking up the house telling her that predators lurked everywhere.

It was truly a beautiful day. There was not a single cloud in the azure blue sky. The air was clear and crisp, and the birds were singing. Rose drove down Short Hill to Highway 21, then took a left down Jane, drove past the pretty Anglican Church on Keith Crescent, and swung onto Sarnia Street.

She then took a left down David Street following the dirt road around the tight bend until it came out in front of the Croquet Club, one of Bayfield's best kept secrets. Indeed, Tom and Rose had lived in their village for five years before either of them had even known about the existence of the club, let alone the geographical whereabouts.

Rose pulled into the car park and immediately saw Mary's blue Honda Civic parked in the car park. Looking out over the immaculately manicured lawns, Rose could see no sign of her friend.

Shrugging her shoulders, she walked over to the storeroom where spare mallets were kept. She opened the cupboard and selected a suitably sized mallet, then poured herself some water and carried it over to the canopied picnic tables.

Where could Mary be? Rose thought and then she saw a mallet lying on the grassy slope leading up to the cemetery which bordered the one side of the Croquet club.

Maybe she's gone to look at the graves, Rose thought as she wandered over to where the mallet lay nestled in the grass. She picked it up and proceeded to walk up to the fence.

All of a sudden Rose spied a piece of white cotton attached to a protruding barb of the fence. Just as her mind was registering the thought that it looked like a piece of material, she saw a foot protruding from behind a gravestone.

Rose carefully climbed over the fence and walked slowly over to where she had seen the foot. She already knew before looking that the shoe on the foot was a white Croc, identical to the one's that Mary always wore for playing croquet.

In silent horror Rose looked at the body of her dear friend slumped over a grey headstone. Her eyes were wide open and her face, even in death, registered a look of sheer terror. A metal arrow had pierced her chest with such force that the tip had literally impaled Mary to the gravestone set in the ground behind her.

Rose stood there numb. It was as if all time stilled into a single, horrific moment. She had not realized it but inadvertently she had held in her breath, and now she exhaled it in one large whoosh. Rose was galvanized into action. Stumbling back to the fence, stepping over it, and running back to the storeroom where she knew there was a phone, out of breath, and still in a state of shock, Rose dialed 911.

Inspector Susan Parker turned left at the junction between Highway 8 and Brucefield. It had been a quick and easy drive from her Richmond Street Major Crimes Unit Headquarters, only one hour and Bayfield, her destination, was a mere 8 minutes away. As she drove on through Varna, Susan started to have mixed feelings about what lay ahead. Last year had been so stressful.

The murder on Bayfield beach and the subsequent uncovering of the Kincardine, Wingham scam, and not forget her disastrous relationship with Jim Reynolds, all served as a jolting reminder to Susan that all was not always what it seemed in the sleepy village of Bayfield.

Initially when she had received the phone call from the OPP detachment outside of Goderich requesting her assistance, Susan had been delighted at the thought of reacquainting herself with the attractively quaint village.

Last year she had discovered that her old university friend, Rose Blair, now lived in the village and the two of them had spent some time catching up on their lives since leaving university. Rose was married to Tom, who, under different circumstances, Susan would have loved to have gotten to know more intimately.

Indeed, there had been that one kiss which had hinted of deeper things, but Tom had firmly attested to his love for his wife, Rose. Susan felt embarrassed remembering the incident and was determined to keep her distance from Tom.

As she reached the ridge at Goshen Line, Susan could see Lake Huron.

The blue water shimmered under the morning sun. Several small sail boats were out. It would be a perfect day for sailing.

She almost missed the turning to the cemetery but, just in time, Susan made the right turn and drove down the leafy, gravel road until she could see an area that had been cordoned off with yellow tape.

There were two O.P.P. cars parked by the side of the tape, and as Susan got out of her car, she could see the body of a woman lying slumped against a gravestone. Two police officers were standing by talking in hushed voices.

"Good morning. My name is Inspector Parker, and you are?" Susan said as she extended her hand to be shaken.

"Oh, I'm Constable Elliot and this is Constable Brown." Both men extended their hands out to shake Susan's.

They don't look old enough to be policemen, flashed through her mind as she shook their hands and then pulled out a pair of white latex gloves. "So, who discovered the body?"

"Er...ma'am, a Mrs. Rose Blair. She is over there the other side of the fence. It's a croquet club."

Susan walked over to the fence and looked onto what appeared to be a bowling green with tightly mown grass. Hoops were placed in a set format.

At the end of the green was a car park where a blue Honda Civic sat alongside a Volvo. Susan recognized the Volvo as her eyes sought the owner whom she knew, Rose Blair.

She saw her friend sitting with her head in her hands under the sun canopy to the left of the croquet court.

"Constable Elliot, walk over and tell Mrs. Blair that she can go home now. Someone will interview her later on today."

Constable Elliot was thirty with a face that looked like a fresh-faced teenager. His hair was buzz cut and his eyes were a startling blue. He nodded his head and set off across the fence to speak to Mrs. Blair.

"Right. Constable Brown, any idea who we have here?" Susan said while still bending over the slumped body.

"Yes, ma'am. Mrs. Blair identified her as one Mary Stokes. She is, um...was, a friend of hers. They were meeting here to practice croquet. The blue Honda belongs to her."

"Thank you, Constable. Forensics should be on their way. Look, I'm going to leave you here while I go into the village to set up an incident room."

Before Susan set off, she took one more look at the dead woman. She was slumped over a gravestone with what looked like a long, metal arrow pierced through her chest. Her face was contorted into a mask of terror. Her legs were bent at an unnatural angle. It looked as if the force of the arrow had literally blown her backwards and impaled her to the stone gravestone.

By the looks of things this had all the signs of a planned execution.

Rose drove home in a daze. Everything felt unreal. Could her friend Mary truly have been murdered at the Croquet Club or was it all just some nasty nightmare and she would awaken from her dream and all would be normal again?

She turned down Charles Street and drove to Bayfield Terrace. As she approached her home with its white picket fence and honeysuckle cascading over the porch, her heart lifted and some of the fog of the morning cleared.

Ben was waiting for her at the door, his tail wagging and big head nudging her for attention. Rose walked into the kitchen and made herself a cup of tea.

She looked at the clock. It was eleven o'clock. She had

been at the Croquet Club for two hours. Tom wouldn't be home until at least one, yet Rose longed to be held in his embrace and to cry on his shoulder.

The shock of finding Mary dead had really impacted Rose's psyche. She just could not wash away the image of Mary's terror etched face, mask like in death.

Rose decided that she would just have to bake away her shock. She started off by making a batch of her cranberry and orange scones and then, for a special treat, she made Ben a tray of liver dog biscuits.

The last baking tray of bone shaped cookies was just coming out of the oven when there was a knock on the door. Ben ambled over and barked just as Rose opened the door.

Susan Parker looked tanned and beautiful wearing a pink, silk blouse tucked into a navy-blue pencil skirt and a matching jacket. Her short, blonde hair from the previous year had grown to a jaw length bob cut which Rose thought was softer and more feminine than the Annie Lennox look that she had sported before.

"Rose, it's been too long. How are you?" Susan hugged Rose warmly and followed her into the kitchen.

"What a delicious smell. I see that you've been baking."

Rose smiled and nodded. "Would you like a cup of coffee and a scone?"

"How could I resist? Yes, I'd love a coffee, but this unfortunately is not a social visit. I'm sure that you know what I've come about?"

Rose felt her eyes well up with tears. For a while she had managed to forget about the horror of the morning, but now she was being faced with the whole ordeal all over again. She took a deep breath and answered softly.

"Yes, Susan, you have to ask me questions about my friend

Mary, but we can do that over a cup of coffee? Here, let's move into the sunroom and I'll bring out the hot buttered scones and coffee."

Rose led Susan into the cozy sunroom. She loved this room. It was the most used area of the house. Susan sat down on one of the soft love seats and Ben immediately jumped up and nestled up beside her resting his big head on her lap.

"Oh Ben, get off you naughty boy." Rose cried.

"I really don't mind, Rose, he's welcome to share the sofa with me. But come on and sit down. I do need to ask you some questions."

Rose placed the tray with a coffee pot, milk jug, two pottery mugs and a plate of buttered Cranberry and orange scones onto the coffee table and then sat down on her favourite cane chair.

"Ok, Susan, fire away."

"Well, we know that the deceased was your friend Mary Stokes and we also know that you were the one that found her. Is there anything else that you can tell us about her? For instance, had she been acting differently or been nervous lately? Had there been any significant change in her behaviour?"

Rose sat still and contemplated her hands and then spoke again with a very small voice.

"I had only known Mary for one year and in that time I felt that I still didn't really know her. She was a very private person. Don't get me wrong, she was lovely, warm, and the most kindhearted woman you're ever likely to meet, but she rarely divulged anything about her past. All I know is that before moving to Bayfield she had lived in Guelph. She was married before, but I know nothing about her previous life."

"We found in her car a purse which carried her driver's

license. We'll be able to track quite a lot down through that but I'm going to set up the incident room first and then I'll send Constable Elliot around to check her house. Did she have any pets?"

Rose let out a small cry. "Oh yes, poor Puff. That's her dog. She loved Puff so much. I'll go around and bring Puff back here. Please don't let him be taken away to the Humane Society. In fact, could you call me when the Constable goes to Mary's house and I'll pop over then and collect Puff?"

"Okay Rose, if you're sure that you don't mind keeping the dog. It doesn't sound as if she had any near or close family around here, but if we find a relative who would like to have the dog then I'm afraid that you will have to relinquish him."

"Of course, I totally understand." Rose said as she handed her over another cup of coffee. Susan departed after demolishing three of the scones and drinking two cups of coffee.

As Rose cleared away the tray and washed up the plates and mugs, she once again had a flashback to her friends' dead body and contorted face. Tears began to roll down her face and a deep sob was wrenched from her throat. Ben, on hearing this, padded over and nudged Rose with his wet nose.

"Oh Benny Boy, I already miss Mary. What happened to my dear friend?"

By the time that Tom arrived home Rose had composed herself, in fact, she got busy again by cooking for the weekend.

Abby and Ella, their darling grandchildren, were coming to stay while Jessica and Rob had a weekend together in Toronto.

She always made 'Grandma's special spaghetti pie' and a dark chocolate and walnut cake when they visited. When Tom entered the kitchen, she was just putting the finishing touches to the cake.

The minute that Rose saw Tom she rushed over to him and said: "Oh Tom, Mary's dead." With that, all resolve for composure went out of the window and Rose once again started to sob. Between great gulps of air, she managed to tell Tom what had happened.

"Poor love," Tom said as he held Rose tightly to his chest and stroked her hair. Ben leaned against Tom's legs, nudging him for attention and for a while the three of them just stood there in silence other than the odd sniff from Rose. Finally, she pulled away from Tom and put on the kettle for some tea. Just then the phone rang, and Tom answered it. As he concluded the conversation he turned to Rose and said, "What's this about collecting Puff?"

Rose bit her lip and said very quietly, "I told Susan that we would look after Puff."

"But what about Ben? How will he feel about us taking in another dog?"

"Oh, Ben will be fine, Tom. Puff is a very friendly dog. He's got some Lab in him. He's a cross between a Labrador and a Golden Retriever. Look, if Ben is too put out by him, I'll look for another home for Puff. But I just know that Mary would have wanted me to look after her beloved dog. Can't you see that?"

"Yes, I suppose so my darling. Anyway, you had better go around to pick up the dog. We'll just have to see how Ben reacts to another dog on his turf."

Mary lived on Christy Street. Rose drove there quickly and parked in front of the small cottage that had been her friend's house. She had spent many hours visiting Mary for coffee over the past year, so Rose was quite familiar with the home. An O.P.P car was parked in the driveway.

Rose knocked on the door which was opened by a handsome and incredibly young-looking officer. He looked vaguely familiar to Rose.

"You must be Rose Blair?" He said. "I'm Constable Elliot, please come in. The dog is in the kitchen."

"Have I met you somewhere before, Constable?" Rose asked as she followed him into the house.

"Oh. Yes, ma'am. I spoke to you at the cemetery earlier today."

Rose nodded as she remembered his kind face as he had told her that she could go home. *I must have looked a real mess,* she thought, recalling her tears.

It seemed odd to be walking through Mary's house without her cheerful voice chatting away. Rose walked past the living room and into the kitchen which was at the back of the house.

Looking around as if for the first time, she realized that there was a distinct absence of photographs anywhere. Compared to Rose's house where they had photographs all over the place, Mary's home seemed strangely devoid of anything personal.

Odd, Rose thought, she had known that her friend was extremely private, but it had never before struck her as strange that there was absolutely no evidence of her past life.

Puff was lying in his dog basket, his golden head resting between his shaggy paws.

"He knows that Mary is dead," Rose said to Constable Elliot. "He just knows."

She collected his dog bowl and clipped on his leash.

"Come on, Puff, let's go home to Ben."

ABOUT THE AUTHOR

Over the past thirty years Judy has written twenty novellas, various collections of poetry and a number of plays. Judy wrote her first full length novel in 2013 and developed it into a series called the Rose Blair Murder Mysteries all set in the sleepy village of Bayfield on the beautiful shores of Lake Huron in Ontario, Canada.

Judy and her husband reside in Bayfield with their beloved dog Susie and cat Thomas and enjoy visits from their children and grandchildren.

After retiring Judy and her husband took on a new challenge in their lives. Purchasing land on the outskirts of Bayfield they have planted a six acre vineyard and are in the process of designing and building a boutique winery.

Life is beautiful and sweet. I feel so very blessed with all my wonderful family and friends who continually surround me with their love.

FIND OUT MORE...

Find Cozy House Press online to read more great cozy mysteries!

www.cozyhousepress.com

COZY HOUSE PRESS
MAKE A DATE WITH MURDER